Our Song

KATE ROWAN

ISBN: 9798669523350

For Mom, my first and greatest fan

&

In loving memory of Popsy

1

Charlie

Adagio, Maine, 1996

I could see my cloudy breath in the cold December air as I curled my trembling hand into a fist and knocked on the door to my grandmother's house, watching as bits of the door's chipped white paint fell to the ground like freshly fallen snow. I felt the tension of six silent years release with the swinging of the door as she answered it. My grandmother flashed me a warm, familiar smile.

That smile escalated into a look of absolute glee, her joy clearly immeasurable. Warmth welled up in my chest, as I knew then and there that I had arrived at home.

"Charlotte," she breathed. "How lovely it is to finally see you again!" She didn't even let me respond before pulling me in for a long, loving embrace. I felt the warmth of her body against mine and felt as if I was transported back in time to the age of eighteen, to the last time I had hugged my dear grandmother.

"Hi, Grandma," I said, a very similar smile appearing now on my own face, "how've you been?"

"Oh, you know..." she began. She trailed off and just stood there for a moment, pride and amazement clearly expressed on her face, which was now etched with lines of worry and age, dulling her youthful glow. "Come with me," she said, putting one arm around me and leading me into the house. "I'll make a pot of tea and we can catch up."

She led me through the house and into the kitchen, where the welcoming scent of vanilla and cinnamon greeted me. She put a tea kettle on the stove and handed me a little homemade biscuit. "Grandma, you don't have to..." I began.

"I insist," she replied, pulling two tiny teacups from the cabinets. After a momentary pause, she continued, "So. How is everything, Dear? I haven't seen you in so very long."

I knew it had been a terribly long time, and I felt positively awful about it. My father had chosen to move away six years prior, when things at home had become too difficult. Staying near Grandpa was just as hard, if not more, than saying goodbye to the man he once was. "I'm so sorry, Grandma. I know I told you I'd see you soon. I should have tried to visit more, I just..." my voice cracked as tears began to fill my eyes and I could no longer find the words to express the thousand emotions flooding my senses. It was true; I hadn't put enough effort into seeing her after the events a few years back, and it plagued me every day.

"Nonsense," my grandmother said, putting down the kettle and wrapping her arms around me in a tight, comforting hug. "It's hard," she breathed into my ear, voice shaking. "I understand. It's really, really hard."

We hugged for a while, the silence filled with unspoken understanding. I pulled away and just gazed into her eyes, as blue and misty as my own. "Thank you."

"Of course," she replied, gathering her composure. "Thank you for coming back to me." She handed me my cup of tea and asked me to follow her.

We soon arrived in her sitting room, adorned with antique paintings of wildflowers and yellowed wallpaper. An old-style lantern rested on a shelf by one of the paintings. I sat on a pastel pink loveseat with a plastic cover on it, and my grandmother sat on an easy chair of the same variety. Instead of a TV and cable box, the center of the room featured an old and ornate grand piano. I remember her telling me stories of my grandfather and how he was the greatest pianist she had ever heard. My memories of his music had begun to fade with time, but it was my greatest wish to someday hear something half as beautiful as my grandmother's descriptions.

"So," she asked me again, "how are you?"

I shifted in my seat, careful not to spill my tea. "I've been pretty great," I said, scrambling to think of an appropriate way to deliver the news that had brought me all the way home to Adagio.

A knowing look teased its way onto her face, as if she knew exactly what I had planned to tell her. "Any news?" She grinned.

"Well, yes." I took a sip of the tea, savoring the heat as it traveled through my chest. It took every ounce of restraint I could muster not to burst. "I have some really good news, actually," I explained instead, feigning relaxed composure.

She shifted forward in her seat, hands in her lap. "What is it?"

I held up my left hand, an elegant diamond ring adorning the fourth finger. In the moments preceding my announcement, I had tried – and failed – to come up with a tactful, polite way to share the news. I couldn't contain myself any longer, though, and simply blurted: "Jonah's asked me to marry him!" I wished I could explain my emotions to her in more detail, but hundreds of different feelings filled me, each one of them more impossible to describe than the last. Instead, I just watched my grandmother.

Her hands flew to her mouth as she gasped. She stood up and rushed over to me, inspecting the ring in finc detail. "It's gorgeous," she whispered softly, as if the vibrations of her voice would damage the precious gem. "Just as I remember it."

After a few moments, her gaze shifted from the ring back to me. Tears filled her eyes. "Tell me everything," she said, her elation teasing a smile onto her lips.

Elation – in a word, that was what I felt. And I knew it was what I would feel every day for the rest of my life.

So, I told her everything, sparing none of the boring details. I told her how we met at college, how I ended up accepting a position teaching high school music in his hometown, the same town to which he had returned to join the family business. I told her how we bonded over our love for music, how he taught me to come out of my shell, how he helped me through my anxieties at college. I was just about to tell her all about how he proposed to me on our fifth anniversary at a reunion concert with his college band, how they played our favorite song as he invited me up on the stage to sing it with him before getting down on one knee, when I noticed tears welling up in her eyes. "What's wrong?" I asked, fearing that something I had said may have upset her.

She shook her head. "Nothing. Nothing's wrong, Dear. It's just..." her voice wavered and she took a deep breath. "Your story reminds me so much of my own."

A strange sense of indescribable pride washed over me, as if she had just given Jonah her stamp of approval. Still, I didn't know why; I had never heard her full story. "I have plenty of time, Grandma," I told her. "Why don't you tell it?"

She stood up and brushed herself off. "Come with me to the kitchen. We'll make some more tea, and I'll tell you everything."

2

Lillian

Adagio, Maine, 1934

Anger fueled my steps as I hiked up my deep blue skirt and trudged down the grandiose staircase leading to the front walkway of my family home, loose strands of my blonde hair whipping in the wind.

Grandiose is a rather subjective term. *Grandiose* in the 1990's and *grandiose* at the height of the Great Depression typically conjure two very different images in my head. *Grandiose* to me, that particular day when I was in such a hurry to get away from my father's estate, meant *proof that we have money, proof that we're just penny-pinching misers in the midst of the worst financial disaster our country has ever seen, proof that we're nothing short of positively despicable.*

Even at the ripe age of twenty, I was still heavily reliant on my father for financial stability, especially as it was extremely difficult for companies anywhere in Adagio to hire new workers, and my father wouldn't allow me to settle for a marriage in which I was the one with the economic upper hand. My father and I disagreed on a lot of issues during my youth, his compulsive need for me to marry into an upper-class family being just one tick in a list with many boxes.

And as I stomped down the stairs that day, our argument still boldly etched in my mind, I decided I no longer had to put up with what my father told me, nor did I have to sit idly by while he told me how to live my life. I would become independent.

"Father, I think it would be best if I start looking for a job. After all, I don't think I'll be fit to marry anytime soon," I had said.

To me, the sentence didn't sound preposterous at all. I was struggling greatly to find a husband of whom my father would approve, and I would eventually need to live on my own, no longer coddled by my overprotective parents, who had spent years teaching me to be a prim and proper lady, just like my perfect success of an older sister, Charlotte.

To my father, on the other hand, my statement was wild and senseless. He argued with me, as he always did when I had ideas of my own. He tried to convince me that I was a fool for thinking I should become employed. After all, I was just a woman. And so, without a second thought, I whirled around, rushing out of the house as my shoes clacked along the pristine white tiles of our foyer floor. Ignoring my father's summons to return to him, I let the door slam behind me and continued on my way.

I didn't really have any plan as to where I was heading or when I would return. The only thing I knew was that I wanted to get out of that house. So that's what I did. The wind began to pick up, as it often did in our little seaside town, and with it came a soft and steady rain shower. I hadn't thought to take an overcoat or umbrella with me when I stormed out, so I took shelter on the nearest stoop, waiting for the storm to pass.

"Hey, Miss," a man's voice beckoned. "Stoop's for paying customers only. In or out."

I glanced once at the door to what seemed to be a rather nice-looking pub, then back at the muddy road and the rain. The choice wasn't difficult; I stood up and followed the man into the establishment.

The interior was nothing like I had expected… Not that I'd had any expectations to begin with, as I had never been inside a pub before. Prohibition had ended a year earlier, but I was still a full year underage. Plus, Mother had always made sure to remind me that a pub was no place for a lady.

It was rather dark inside, a few sconces on the walls being the sole illumination. The bar was at the front, and other seating was spread throughout the room. There were only a few customers in the whole place; a couple at the end of the bar, and an older man sitting at a booth towards the back. I figured that the recent financial crisis must've been keeping most customers away. A grand piano sat amidst the tables and there was an open area which I assumed was meant for dancing. There was a man at the piano, filling the room with his soft music, but his gaze was distant, his mind clearly elsewhere.

"I'd like an alcoholic drink," I said firmly, taking a seat at the bar, confident that the bartender would oblige.

Instead, he stopped what he was doing and fixed his gaze upon me. He raised one eyebrow and a smile crept onto his face. "Absolutely not." Upon noticing my bewildered expression, he continued. "If you leave now, I won't let your father know you were here."

"How do you know my father?" My voice shook as I wondered how my scheming father had swindled this poor man.

"Miss, everyone knows your father. You're an Abbott. High cheekbones, bright blue eyes and looking fairly put together? There's no doubt in my mind. Your family's the richest in town."

When I didn't respond, he continued. "Your father's in real estate, yes?"

I nodded.

The man grumbled in response. "That nogoodnik sold me this property about seven years ago, helped me open my business. I was thankful, of course, but he charged me way too much for what I was getting. Didn't tell me the lighting only worked half of the time and the storage area was growing mold. Ended up costing me a fortune in renovations, right before the crash. And now, well... Business isn't exactly booming. A few more weeks like this and I'll be bankrupt." The man scoffed and took out a rag, wiping down the bar, avoiding my apologetic gaze.

"Well, Sir, I'm very sorry you had to deal with all of that..." I began, my tone sincere, but the man cut me off.

"Do you *realize* how much of my life he stole from me?" The man pounded his fist down on the bar, rattling the half-empty glasses on the other end. His cheeks flushed red and the vein on his forehead was growing ever larger.

"I-I..." My body was frozen, I didn't know if I should try to leave or reason with the man, who continued to get angrier by the second.

"Do you?" His voice boomed as he came around the bar and advanced towards me. My heart thrummed loudly in my chest and I could feel the heat in my cheeks. I tried to stand and leave, but my long skirt was caught under the leg of the barstool and I fell to my knees with a gasp.

The piano playing suddenly stopped as the man behind it rose from his bench and approached the bartender. "Excuse me, Sir," the pianist said calmly, his voice smooth and lyrical.

The bartender pulled his eyes from me and faced the musician. "And what can I do for you, young man?"

"You can leave this poor woman alone." The pianist knelt down and offered his arm, helping me to my feet. I brushed myself off and looked up to thank him, but his sharp green eyes were glued to the bartender.

"Mister Quinn," said the bartender, "I hope you understand what's at stake here – I let you into my fine establishment, I let you play that piano day in and day out. You'd do best not to cross me."

"You'd do best not to hurt an innocent young lady," he retorted boldly.

I gasped, and, suddenly, my feet were glued to the floor. I watched, frozen, my eyes following the bartender's fist as it flew over the bar and hit its mark with faultless precision. The pianist doubled over and blood splashed onto the bottom of my skirt.

3

Charlie

Pine Ridge University, 1990

I finished taping up the last poster on my dorm room wall and turned to look at my parents, standing teary-eyed in the doorway. I looked down at my feet, then back at them: my father, wearing his signature plaid shirt, scratching the scruffy stubble he had recently decided to grow out, with his arm wrapped around my mother, a petite redhead with a stern look about her. In that moment, I couldn't help but think that I was the perfect blend of the both of them. I had my mother's studious, cautious personality, and my dad's bright blue eyes and big heart. "One more?" I asked.

My mother gave a gentle nod and I rushed into their arms for one final hug before they would leave me. "See you in six weeks," I said.

"See you soon." My dad pulled away and gave me a comforting look. The light slanting through the window cast a glare on his circular glasses as he pushed them further up the bridge of his nose. "You're gonna be great."

"Make sure you call," my mom reminded me.

I looked up into her friendly brown eyes and smiled. "Of course, I will," I assured her.

"And don't get into any trouble," she repeated for the third time as my father ushered her out the door.

I giggled and waved to them as they left, leaving me in my freshman dorm all alone for the very first time. My giddy smile slowly faded, my face falling as I looked around the empty room, a newfound loneliness settling deep in my chest. I sat on my freshly made bed, the thin mattress letting out a little puff of air as I collapsed into it. I don't remember crying, but I'm sure I did.

I looked out the window just in time to see my parents rounding the corner, away from the building, and out of my sight for the next two and a half months. The pit in my stomach reminded me that I'd never been on my own for more than a weekend before, but the motivational sticky notes my RA had left on my door told me that I could do it. Sucking in a deep breath, I decided to believe the RA.

I was determined to have a successful college experience. I would get good grades, have reliable friends, and make connections so I'd get great jobs in the future. I'd make sure to keep my scholarship and I wouldn't get into *any* trouble. I'd make my parents proud.

I lived a quiet, sheltered life in high school. I'd never tasted a sip of alcohol, never had a boyfriend. I had a perfect GPA and was involved in student council and lots of service clubs. My mom was a bit overbearing, I'll admit, but I loved her all the same. She just wanted what was best for me. I planned to make her proud, to maintain my good reputation through my years in college, just like I did in high school… Though I wasn't quite sure how to do that in this new setting.

Aspen Hall, room 428, I repeated to myself as I grabbed my key, student ID, and wallet and took a glance in the mirror, gathering my confidence. My roommate hadn't yet arrived, so I figured it would be okay to wander around campus for a while until she did. Getting an idea for the layout of the campus would help to ensure I wouldn't be late to any of my classes during the chaos of the first week.

As a first-generation student, I had a lot to prove. I couldn't let anything get in the way of my studies, for fear I'd lose my scholarship. Determination coursed through my veins. I tied my auburn waves into a ponytail and exited Aspen Hall.

It was move-in day, and campus was bustling with activity. Students were tossing a football back and forth on a lawn in the distance, people sat on benches eating burgers and hot dogs. Groups of orientation leaders in matching t-shirts chanted loudly, trying to get all of the new students excited about their first weekend. I wondered if campus would always be this way – full of life and energy. In the distance, I could hear live music being played. As a music education major, I had no choice but to go check it out.

The band was made up of five slightly older-looking boys – a lead singer, two guitarists, a bassist and a drummer. Basically, they looked like the epitome of a wannabe hippie boy band. I hated to admit it, but they pulled it off rather well. I could feel their music pulsating in my chest as I got closer, the lead singer belting out the lyrics to "Cover Girl" by New Kids on the Block.

A rather large group of students had ended up surrounding them, and before I knew it, I was involved in some sort of outdoor move-in day dance party on the field behind Somerset Hall, and, boy, would that be a moment to remember. Slightly uncomfortable but very intrigued, I bounced my way closer to the stage, shoving through the crowds of people so I could see the band.

I was immediately drawn to the bassist. I noticed his fingers first, calloused and tough from years of perfecting his craft. He moved them methodically, rhythmically, perfectly – lightning precision in perfect time. I couldn't help but be impressed – I had been playing the violin since age four and always admired someone who knew their way around a set of strings.

I wanted to go up and tell him just how impressed I was, but there was a huge mob of girls rushing towards him when they finished their set. I knew I didn't want to get involved in that mess, so I opted to walk around the other way.

I caught his eye on my way back to my own dorm and flashed him a quick smile. He winked at me as he toyed with the green bandana tied on his head full of brown waves.

Feeling strangely warm on my walk back to Aspen Hall, room 428, I realized that in my first few hours on campus I had done just what I swore I wouldn't do – I had become distracted.

By my future fiancé, no less.

4

Lillian

Adagio, Maine, 1934

"Out! Both of you, out of my pub!" the bartender hollered.

It was as if I had just snapped out of a trance. I gathered up the front of my dress and pulled the pianist to his feet. We rushed out the door as the bartender launched a glass in our direction. I made sure to shut the door behind us, just as the glass smashed against its wooden frame.

"Are you alright?" he asked me, his voice laced with concern.

I nodded. "You aren't, though," I observed, reaching a hand to his injured face.

He flinched away from me. "I'll be fine." He tenderly brushed his finger against the cut above his eyebrow, where the bartender's wedding ring lacerated his skin, fresh blood dripping from the wound.

"You may need stitches," I insisted. "My older brother is a medical student, let him look at it."

After a few more moments of stubbornness on both of our parts, the pianist finally allowed me to take him to meet Benjamin, my eldest brother.

"Thank you," I said quietly, a few minutes into the walk.

"It was nothing, really." His voice was cool and calm, but I could see a twinkle of pride in his eyes as he spoke. "I'm Henry, by the way. Henry Quinn."

"Lillian."

We arrived at the front gate to my father's huge estate, and I turned to Henry. "We just have to hope my father isn't in the foyer – then we should be able to sneak right into Ben's room without him noticing."

Henry remained at the gate for a few moments, wide-eyed. "You live *here*?"

"Unfortunately."

It took a few more moments for him to collect himself and speak again. “Wow… And we have to hide from your father because...?”

“He and I… Have our differences.”

He gave a deliberate nod and I pushed open the gate. As we hurried across the front lawn to the door, Ben appeared on the porch. “Lillian, what on Earth is going on? Who is this?”

Henry offered his hand to my brother. “My name’s Henry,” he said.

Ben ignored his outstretched hand and took a brief look at his eye. “Come in.” He took a breath. “I’ll fix you up, and Lillian can explain everything to me.” He shot me a look and my blue eyes met his own with indignance.

We led Henry through the foyer, around the corner and into the kitchen. Ben pulled up a chair, instructed the injured pianist to sit, and began preparing to address the injury. He placed his supplies on the limestone counter, moving Mother’s collection of pots and pans out of the way and started sorting through bandages and salves.

“I’m so sorry for any inconvenience I’m causing,” Henry said. “Your sister…” He trailed off when he noticed Ben and I were lost in our own bickering, neither of us paying him any attention.

"Lillian, what have I told you about allowing strangers in?"

"I know, I just-"

"Where did you find him, anyway?"

"He helped me, I was-"

"And why did you need helping? What sort of trouble-"

"Father and I had been fighting, and I-"

Ben interrupted me with a harsh sigh and began applying a salve to Henry's eye. "Thank you," Henry tried again to express his gratitude.

"I'm sorry you had a fight with Father, but…" Ben trailed off, resigned, then, after a moment, collected himself and continued. "You really mustn't run off like that, Lily."

I chose to ignore my older brother's scolding. "How's your eye feeling, Henry?" I asked.

"Much better already." He turned to Ben. "Your sister is too kind, offering such help."

"Don't mention it," Ben said coldly. He walked over to the kitchen sink and washed his hands.

"Lily?"

I heard the high-pitched voice echo from the top of the steps. "I'm down here, Mary," I called to my youngest sister.

I could hear the soft pitter of her tiny feet as she rushed down the stairs to give me a big hug. I knelt down and wrapped her in my arms, giving her a kiss on the cheek. "How was your day, Mary?"

"It was good! Mother and I tended the garden for a while, but then it started to rain, so I had to go inside and get washed up."

At only eight years old, Mary was as innocent and wise as they come. She spent her days playing in the garden and exploring the halls of our large house, learning more and more each day. I envied her, wishing that she would never have to grow up and face the cold, bitter truth of reality.

Her eyes widened when she saw Henry. "Who's that?" she asked me quietly.

"His name is Henry," I whispered back to her. "He's a friend, but you mustn't tell Mother or Father he's come around, okay?"

Mary nodded slowly, her strawberry blonde curls bouncing up and down. "He's very handsome," she pointed out, her voice scarcely a whisper, her eyes glued to Henry's chiseled features.

"He'll be our little secret," I continued with a playful wink.

"Our secret," Mary agreed.

Henry stood and shook Ben's hand, preparing to leave. I walked him out and we crossed the front lawn side by side. We paused when we reached a large tree at the edge of our property. He looked down at me, a single strand of his deep brown hair straying from the rest. He tucked it away and began, "Thank you for everything today, it was a pleasure. Well, despite the… you know."

"No, thank you," I responded, blushing. "I hope I'll see you again someday." I twirled a piece of blonde hair between my two fingers and looked down at my feet, suddenly conscious of my appearance.

A shy smile appeared on Henry's face for a split second before he cleared his throat and adjusted his posture. "Likewise."

He disappeared behind the gate and my stomach dropped. It was then that I realized I *really* wanted to see him again.

Regardless, I returned to the house and was greeted by my mother, who asked me to help her fix dinner. I spoke no word of Henry or his presence in our home. Thankfully, my siblings remained silent as well, though I could feel the judgment of my overprotective brother in his gaze.

5

Charlie

Pine Ridge University, 1990

It was 8:00 on a Monday morning, the first day of classes, and there I sat in a random seat in the middle of a tiny, insignificant lecture hall somewhere in a building I have since forgotten, leaning against the back of my chair, sipping bitter coffee from my dad's old travel mug. It was all I could do to keep my eyes open after the rigorous orientation exercises of the previous weekend. I laid my books out in front of me, sending a silent prayer up to the sky that I would pass my first ever college course here in this very seat.

It was Music Theory 101.

And three minutes after class started, one of those hippie boy band wannabes waltzed into the room and sunk into the empty chair to my left, the sound of his chewing gum so loud that I'm sure the professor could hear it all the way at the podium.

"Hey," he whispered to me.

I chose not to acknowledge him, and instead played with the seam on my ruffled floral skirt.

"Hey," he said again, tossing an unruly blond curl behind his ear with a swift flick of his neck. The sound of his gum got louder.

"Hi," I whispered shyly, worried that the professor would see us fooling around and call us out in the middle of his lecture.

"Whatcha doing tonight?"

"Probably studying," I said. I still hadn't made eye contact with the boy. I refused to let him get between me and my schoolwork.

"Damn shame," he noted. "You should come to my band's gig. I'm the drummer. Name's Shane." He tapped his pencil against the edge of his desk as if to impress me.

"I'm Charlie," I told him, "and I suppose it is." I returned my attention to the class. *Circle of fifths,* I thought to myself. *We're studying the circle of fifths.*

"It's in Aspen common room," he said. "You're a freshman, right? Know anyone who lives there?"

Circle of fifths, circle of fifths!

"I do." *Why did I tell him that?*

"Then I'd better see you there." Shane gave me a playful wink and returned his attention to tapping his pencil on the desk.

I seriously doubt that, I thought to myself. "Maybe." *What are you doing, Charlie?*

Once the professor brought my first college lecture to a close, I couldn't have been more grateful. Attention was not my strong suit that day. I only hoped I would be able to do better in the future.

I walked out of class quickly, before most students even had the chance to gather their books. I wasn't quite sure why I kept telling Shane I might go see his band. I already had a hot date planned – with the circle of fifths.

"Tonight at eight!" Shane hollered across the hall on his way out of the building. "Aspen Commons! Be there!"

I rolled my eyes and pushed open the heavy double door, breathing in the fresh morning air as I pulled out the folded piece of paper from my pocket. I stopped at a nearby bench shaded by maple trees and tried to make sense of where I was to go next. "Music Theory 101…" I muttered under my breath. "okay, in half an hour I have a violin lesson." I straightened my watch and stood up, deciding I would have enough time for another cup of coffee before my lesson.

Luckily for me, there was a little coffee shop right next to the music building, where all of my lectures and practices would take place. It was called Café Harmony, and the inside was decorated with cute paintings of instruments and scattered with tea lights for ambiance. "Medium hot vanilla latte, please," I said to the worker.

He handed me a cup just a few moments later, but his fingers slipped and soon I was wearing a medium hot vanilla latte all over my white shirt and floral skirt. "I'm so sorry, miss, I'll make you a new one, I…" his voice quieted and he looked away from me. "Aye, my man! Cream and cinnamon?"

My eyes widened as I looked up to see the bandana-wearing bassist from Shane's band sauntering towards the coffee stand. My cheeks were suddenly hot and I turned away from him, busying myself with trying to wipe the coffee-colored stains from my white shirt.

"You got it, Alex," he responded to the worker. An awkward moment of silence filled only by the whirring of the coffee maker lingered between us, until eventually he broke it. "You were at the concert on Friday, right?"

I looked up at him and crossed my arms over my chest, trying to hide the ugly brown stain I was wearing. "Um, yeah, I was. You were brilliant."

I gazed into his honey-colored eyes for a moment before he hurriedly removed his backpack. "Uh, here," he said, setting down his bass case and rummaging through a plethora of random items within the bag. He handed me a grey t-shirt with a faded logo on it. 'For Madeleine,' it read.

"We were supposed to wear these for a gig tonight, but I think you need it more than I do." He gestured to my coffee-stained top. "It's tonight at eight in Aspen Commons." He grabbed the coffee that was waiting for him and handed me my second vanilla latte of the morning. "Hope to see you there." His eyes caught mine for just a split second before he pulled away and rushed out the door.

I still didn't know his name.

6

Lillian

Adagio, Maine, 1934

"It's delicious, Mother, thank you," Ben said, taking another spoonful of carrots from the bowl in the center of our dining table.

"You're welcome, Benny. Your sister helped, too." Mother winked at me and I smiled. Looking at my mother was like looking in a mirror. Her beautiful blonde curls rested gently along her shoulders, her soft features growing more delicate with age. I admired her more than anyone. She was strong, resilient, and so very brave.

Ben smiled and locked eyes with Mary. "Mary, your cooking is delightful."

"I don't even know how to work a stove!" Mary hollered, erupting in laughter.

I smiled at Ben, knowing that he had already forgiven me for my mistakes with Henry, and he returned it kindly. Nearly our whole family was sitting around the table, as they were every evening. The only person missing was my sister Charlotte, who had recently moved in with her husband, Norman.

Father sat at the head of the table, with Mother directly to his left and Ben to the right. I was seated next to Mother, across from my two younger brothers, Robert, who was seventeen, and eleven-year-old Samuel. Mary sat to my right.

"Did everyone have an exciting day?" Father's voice echoed in the dining room, sending a chill down my spine.

I nodded tentatively, praying Ben and Mary wouldn't give me away. Ben glanced in my direction and said, "Not much for me. I heard–" my heart skipped a beat – "Mary had a great time in the garden with Mother." I let out a sigh of relief.

Mary nodded excitedly. "Oh, yes, I did!"

"Matthew was telling me about his new job, Father," Robert said.

"Don't you get any ideas, young man," my father replied. "I expect you'll be mature enough to start working with me in just a few months."

"Yes, father."

His attention shifted from my brother to me. "Lillian," he inquired, "how was the rest of your day spent?"

Every muscle in my body tensed. I knew better than to lie to Father, but there was no sense in telling the truth. I had already angered him once that day, and I didn't plan to make that mistake twice. "I read a bit, wrote in my journal."

"And what did you write about?"

I was terrified he'd catch me in the lie. "I wrote a poem."

"About?"

"Uh, bluebirds." *Don't ask to read it,* I willed, *don't ask me to go get it.*

"I'd love to read it, once dinner finishes."

Damn.

"I'll see if I can find it," I said, hoping to find some way out of this mess.

"I'd hope you could, as you just wrote it today."

I took a bite of the chicken Mother and I prepared, busying myself with the food so I wouldn't have to reply with more than a slight nod.

After dinner, when father asked me to go retrieve the poem, my mind scrambled as I thought of what I could do to cover up my thoughtless error. I knew I couldn't write one on the spot; Father new my best poetry too well to consider one I pondered for just a moment as good as one I'd spent the whole day writing. Instead, I tore a blank page out of my journal and showed him the space where my "poem" used to be.

Of course, it took a lot more than that to fool the man who fools for a living.

I held the journal against my chest as I glided back down the stairs, my heart beating against my ribs. Father was waiting in the sitting room with a sly smile toying at the corners of his mouth.

"I know you're lying to me," he said to me after I explained my story. His voice was a quiet hiss, his breath hot in my ear.

I shook my head vigorously. *Don't cry, don't cry, don't cry.*

His hand was a blunt hammer against my arm as he whirled me around and threw me onto the floor, the rough material of the sitting room rug grating against my skin. "To your room."

"Father, I..." my voice cracked as a tear fell from my eye.

"I'll see you there soon, and I trust you'll tell me the truth at that time."

I wiped the tear from my face and hurried to my feet. I walked swiftly up to my room, staring downward as I ascended the staircase. I sat on my bed and waited for the inevitable, my heart thrumming rapidly against my chest.

My father entered quietly, gently, as he always did. He shut my door behind him and sat beside me on my bed. His large arm wrapped itself around my waist and I flinched. "Now, Lillian," he said, an eerie calmness lining his voice, "why don't you tell me what you did today?"

"Nothing," I responded, refusing to look him in the eyes.

In an instant, his arm was no longer wrapped around me, but tossing my petite figure across the room. Pain seared through my body as I crashed into my oak dresser. I could feel sharp, hot tears burning my eyes, but I refused to let them escape. I knew crying would only make me appear weaker.

He hurdled towards me, the suited, charming businessman suddenly transformed into some sort of rabid animal, and I darted from one corner of my room to the other, ignoring the pain he had inflicted.

He eventually reached me.

I envied Charlotte. She had escaped.

I feared for Mary. I feared she would grow up.

Tomorrow, I would have to sew the buttons back on my dress.

7

Charlie

Aspen Hall, 1990

When I got back to my dorm that evening, I caught sight of myself in the mirror and was reminded that I was still wearing the grey t-shirt that the bassist had given me. It was at least two sizes too big, hanging down nearly to my knees and covering most of my skirt. I changed into a different top as my roommate, Ruby, entered the room. "Hey," she said.

"Hey," I responded. "Did you still want to see that band tonight? They're playing in the common room in..." I glanced at my watch – "eight minutes."

Ruby pondered the thought for a moment. "Absolutely," she decided. "I heard they're, like, insanely hot."

I blushed and let out a soft laugh. "I mean, they're not bad," I replied sheepishly.

I could see an excited glint in her eye. "Give me ten minutes to get ready."

"Okay," I said. After a pause, I continued, suddenly getting nervous about pushing off my homework until the next day. "I wasn't gonna go, originally."

"How could you miss it? Five hot guys playing live music in the same building you live in?"

I sighed and hopped onto my bed while Ruby changed from her sweats into a high waisted denim skirt and a flowy yellow top. "I guess you're right," I replied. "I mean, I told the one that I would go so I could return his shirt."

One of the sandals Ruby was pondering fell to the ground. She turned to me, wide-eyed. "You *know* them? Aren't they like the coolest kids on campus? You're a *freshman.* We moved in, like, ten minutes ago."

"Five days ago, actually," I said, retrieving her sandal from the floor and putting it back in her delicately manicured hand. "Now, hurry up, if you want to see them!"

As she stood at the mirror applying a thick layer of mauve lipstick, I couldn't help but be envious. Ruby was absolutely stunning. Tawny curls sat atop her head, tied up by a floral headband, a few delicate strands framing her soft-featured face.

"Okay," she said, taking one last glance in the mirror before grabbing her keys. "Ready?"

I nodded and followed her out. We went down the hall and to the left, into the elevator. By the time the elevator reached the third floor, we could feel the vibrations of the music through our thinly soled shoes. Once we hit the ground floor, it pulsated through our entire bodies. The bass resonated in my chest, sending a chill down my spine. Ruby looked at me, excitement written all over her face, and I bounced up and down, clutching the grey t-shirt with both hands.

The elevator doors slid open to reveal a huge crowd of people in my very own common room, most of whom I had never seen before, and would probably never see again. In the center of the room, the five boys had created a makeshift stage out of our study tables. On the chalkboard behind them, someone had written "For Madeleine – LIVE!" in big, loopy handwriting. People were standing on couches, others on chairs, and some were just dancing for all it was worth.

Shane saw Ruby and I enter, and he gave me a nod from behind his drum set. I waved back. Ruby shook me. "Oh my god, he really does know you!" she exclaimed.

"I know!" I replied, shouting over the music. "I had no idea they were this popular!"

"This is insane! They're amazing!"

I nodded and she grabbed my hand, leading me through the crowd of people. We eventually made it up to the cluster of tables they were using as a stage. When they finished their song, the bassist sat down, his legs dangling off the edge of the table, and took a sip of his water bottle. "Hey," I said, approaching him.

"Hey."

"I brought your shirt back." I held it out to him.

"Thanks." He took it and removed his own. I had to make a conscious effort not to stare at his gorgeous abs. I tried to share a look with Ruby, but she, too, seemed to be distracted by his shirtless-ness.

"Hi," my roommate said, her voice honeyed and flirty. She took a step closer, standing between the bassist and myself. "I'm Ruby."

"Jonah," he replied. He craned his neck to look at me. "I don't think I caught your name earlier…"

"Charlie," I told him.

He smiled at the both of us. It was charming, I had to admit, but I was well-aware that the only love affairs I would embark upon during that semester would be with my Music Theory textbooks. "We're having a party after this, over in the suite houses. Not many people know about it, but you two should come – I'll make sure you get in."

"Oh, I don't know," I said sheepishly, suddenly anxious about the thought of going to a party. I hadn't even planned on staying at the gig. "I've got class in the morning, and I-"

"I'll be there," Ruby said quickly, putting her hand on his leg. She gave him a wink and walked off.

"It's a shame you can't come," he said to me. "But I'll see you around, right?"

"Actually, I think I will come," I said, glancing back at Ruby as she made her way through the crowd.

"What about your class?"

"It'll be fine." *What are you doing?* I thought to myself, *you're supposed to be focusing on classes, working to keep your scholarship so you can stay here!*

"You sure?"

"Yeah."

"Dope. Tell your friend and find me after, we'll walk over together."

I nodded and walked off as he stood up and joined his bandmates to start their last song of the night – an original written by the lead singer, named Cedar, in honor of his ex-girlfriend. His unruly mop of bright red hair bounced to the beat of the music as he passionately begged for her to take him back.

About six minutes later, after a mildly embarrassing, yet somewhat riveting emotional performance by Cedar, the three of us were together again, walking out of Aspen Hall in the direction of the upperclassmen's housing. Ruby and Jonah walked side by side, and I lingered a few paces behind, still not sure of why I was on my way to a party on a Monday night. It wasn't my scene – I had never even been to a party before. Why was I so intrigued?

Various colors of neon lights flashed in the open windows of the suite house, dance music tearing through the silence of the night. My stomach twisted into a knot and a sudden sense of unease fell over me. Something deep down told me the party would be bad news. I belonged in a coffee shop with a book in my hands or in the music building with my violin, not at a party full of extroverts and alcohol. "Ruby," I called for my roommate's attention.

She turned around at the sound of my voice. "Charlie," she replied. "What's the matter?"

As she got closer to me, I said to her quietly, "I don't think I should be here."

"Look," she said, grabbing my shoulders and looking into my eyes with her beautiful amber ones. "I know you're not used to this. I know you're scared. But college is all about trying new things." She paused, then leaned in close. "Plus, I'm totally gonna bang this guy tonight," she whispered in my ear, gesturing to Jonah, who was standing in front of the door to the suite house with his hands in his pockets, swaying mindlessly to the music.

Ruby and I returned to his side and the three of us walked in together. I had a sinking suspicion I would regret the decision.

8

Lillian

Adagio, Maine, 1934

Ben appeared in my doorway just moments after Father had left. He gave me a knowing look and entered my room slowly, cautiously. Neither of us said a word while he propped up his medical kit on my nightstand and began preparing his supplies.

He came over to my bed and sat beside me, examining the ugly purple bruise on my shoulder. "What was it this time?"

"The dresser," I said, motioning to the oak furniture I had collided with. I bit my lip, trying to hold back the tears burning my eyes.

Ben nodded and began fixing me up. "Are you hurt anywhere else? How's your wrist?"

"No, I'm alright," I replied, rotating my right hand to demonstrate that the injury he had helped me with last time had healed properly.

"Good." He stood up and gathered his things. "If you need anything else, let me know, Lily. I love you."

"I love you too, Ben," I said, voice cracking. "Thank you." A tear rolled down my cheek and I brushed it away as Ben shut the door softly behind him.

I stood up slowly, my body aching, and walked over to my mirror. My injuries weren't too noticeable, save for a rather nasty-looking split lip. I stared at it for a moment, trying to think of a reasonably believable lie to tell if anyone asked about it. I knew that it was my duty to help uphold my father's reputation, no matter how much we… fought.

I took a deep breath and headed to the bath, more than ready to cleanse my body of my father's sins. I locked the door behind me and let my dress slip off my shoulders and onto the floor. A chill ran down my body as I sank into the warm water, and I let out a sigh of relief. *Peace*.

I allowed my mind to wander for a few moments and thoughts of Henry slipped into my head. Our experience earlier that day had been terrifying, sure, but something about it was such a joy. I had finally been able to indulge my sense of adventure... And my father still hadn't a clue.

Still, when I thought of Father, a strong, uncomfortable pain arose from deep within me, a pain I could never quite shake, a pain that would always follow me, that would always burn me, scar me. He would always be there, and he would never be there; he was no more than an empty chasm of anger where there could have been a heart.

When I decided that I'd had enough of the bath, I wrapped myself in a towel and headed for bed. It was only just past eight, but that particular day had provided enough excitement to last a week or more. I climbed into my bed and tried not to let any invasive thoughts creep into my head.

I dreamed of adventure, of high spirits and excitement. I dreamed that I had no fear, that I had traveled far away and that my father would never find me.

I dreamed of Henry, of the adventures we could have together and the moments we could share.

And then I woke up, disappointed that none of what I had dreamt was real. It was a Saturday, which meant I would have to accompany my mother to harvest vegetables from our garden. I rose from my bed and got dressed in an old red and white polka-dotted day dress.

"Morning, Mother," I said, arriving in the kitchen.

Mother had just finished pouring Mary a glass of water. "Good morning, Dear," she replied. "I'm fixing some eggs for Mary; would you care for any?"

"That would be lovely." I watched as she reached for the pot, wincing as she burned the tip of her finger. "Here, let me help." I took a wooden spoon and a potholder from the drawer and got to work, trying to avoid eye contact with my mother so she wouldn't see my split lip.

My mother knew of the tainted relationship I had with my father. It was rather difficult to keep something of such a nature from a mother – they always seem to know when something is wrong… Still, I hated to see her worry. I did all I could to keep her and my younger siblings sheltered from the things he would put me through behind closed doors. She was a brave woman, my mother, but I could hardly bear to see the first time she realized Father had been hurting his daughters. I wondered what it must have been like to find out that the man she loved with all her heart and soul was a man without a heart and soul of his own.

"Thank you," she replied. She left the kitchen and I could hear her calling Mary as I finished up the cooking. I seasoned my sister's breakfast with some pepper and set it on the table for her.

"Good morning, Mary," I said to her, making a conscious effort to sound as cheerful as possible and ignore the throbbing pain in my shoulder, "how did you sleep?"

"Great!" the little girl replied, digging into her eggs.

After breakfast, the three of us went out into the garden to collect tomatoes, carrots, cucumbers and peppers. Ben would be spending the weekend catching up on schoolwork, Father was out working, and I was sure Robert would be outside with his best friend, enjoying his last few days of childhood before his birthday, when father would ask him to join the family real estate business.

We had only been outside for a few minutes when I saw a dark flash out of the corner of my eye. "I'll be right back," I said quietly to Mary, who was rather preoccupied with a stubborn carrot.

I approached the corner of our shed, where I saw the blur. "Hello?" I called gently.

No answer.

"Is anyone there?" I rounded the corner. "I'm not going to hurt you," I added.

A boy's head peeked out from behind a nearby bush. His mop of dark hair and light eyes reminded me remarkably of Henry, but he couldn't have been older than fourteen or fifteen. "You don't have to be afraid," I said.

He still said nothing, but crawled out from his hiding place, revealing a pile of tomatoes he had been trying to hide in his dirt-stained white shirt. Tears began filling his eyes. "I'm sorry miss, I know I shouldn't have…"

I approached him slowly, putting a gentle hand on his shoulder. "It's okay," I said. "I understand." I lowered my voice to a hushed whisper. "Take them out through the back gate, so no one sees you." A pause. "Good luck."

"Lillian!" I heard my sister call.

"Coming, Mary!" I hollered back. "Go!" I urged the boy, and turned away from him, heading back around the shed and back to my family.

"What was that?" my mother asked.

"Just a rabbit," I lied. "A very hungry, determined little rabbit."

9

Charlie

Pine Ridge University, 1990

"I'm ready," I told Ruby, and the two of us walked up to meet Jonah before we went into the suite party. Upon entering, my senses were assaulted by the sharp, hot smell of alcohol, the sight of what seemed to be a thousand writhing bodies, and the deafeningly loud music. Ruby and I exchanged looks and shrugged before following Jonah deeper into the party, where he met up with Shane, Cedar, and the other two band members, Otto and Declan.

I tried bouncing up and down to the beat of the music, but I was feeling so beyond claustrophobic in that moment. I was suffocating in the mass of sweaty people. Trying my best to get a sense of my surroundings, I eventually caught sight of Ruby, sitting on a flimsy metal chair in the corner of the room. I started to make my way towards her, but soon realized that she wasn't the only one in the chair. Jonah's hands crept his way up her shirt as they sat there together, completely engulfed in their own little world, and I turned away, rather disgusted.

I'm totally gonna bang this guy tonight, Ruby's voice echoed in my head, causing my stomach to churn. In a way, I felt bad for Jonah. Did he know he was about to be nothing more to her than a one-night stand?

"You've got to try this!" Shane appeared behind me with a drink in his hand. "Here." He gave it to me, and I took a cautious sip. The bitter taste burned my mouth and throat.

"What is this?" I asked, making a face.

"Straight vodka, baby!"

"Oh, God," I said, putting the cup down. "It's terrible!"

Shane shrugged.

I jumped and a rush of adrenaline surged through my body as a loud crash interrupted our conversation. Curses flew from Shane's mouth and he charged across the room, through the crowd of people and towards the source of the sound.

"What's going on?" he hollered, arriving at what appeared to be a rather savage fight.

There were two guys standing by the wall. One of them leaned against it and the other had fallen to the ground and was clutching what looked like a badly dislocated shoulder. "He said that I was the one who kissed his Alice, but I didn't, she just was like, 'kiss me' but I swear I didn't do it…" My head started to ache as I struggled to understand his drunken ramblings. I shot a puzzled look at Shane, hoping he would know what to do.

"Okay, somebody must've found the Aftershock," Shane said, catching the guy who spoke right before he hit the floor. He motioned to me and I helped to hold him upright. The two of us sat him on a bench. "You stay here with Luke," Shane instructed, "I'll go get Jonah. He's always sober enough for this stuff. He'll know what to do."

He left me alone with Luke and the other drunk guy. I sat on the bench and every muscle in my body tensed. This was all… Very new to me.

A few moments later, Shane returned with Jonah, who clearly wasn't as drunk as most of the other people at the party. I finally felt like I could relax when he arrived, somehow knowing I was safe. "Hey, Luke," Jonah said to the drunk guy. He sat down on his left, and I remained to his right.

"Wait a minute," I said, trying to get Jonah's attention as he held out a plastic trash can for Luke, rubbing his back.

"Hmm?" He looked up at me with his light brown eyes.

"Where's Ruby?"

"Jonah!" Her voice echoed through the crowd as she appeared, making her way through the mass of people.

His attention snapped away from me and onto my roommate. Her legs swayed beneath her as she stumbled towards him. "Hi, Rubes," he said awkwardly, handing me Luke's trash can and standing up to support the imbalanced weight of my intoxicated roommate.

"Hello, Jonah," she said, her words running together. I rolled my eyes. I was starting to think that coming to this party was a mistake. Ruby squeezed his arm and whispered something inaudible in his ear.

I could see his eyes widen, and he shook his head. "No," he said, "no, I don't think that's a good idea right now."

I gave him a confused look.

"Let's get you back to Aspen," Jonah continued. Ruby leaned more of her weight against him and he scooped her up in his arms. She toyed with his hair and mumbled something I couldn't quite discern.

My breath hitched and my heartbeat accelerated. "I'll take her back," I said to him, handing Luke his trash can and standing up.

"I can't let you take her alone. We'll go together." He looked Ruby in the eyes. "Ruby?" he said softly. "Can you walk?"

She nodded and we each supported her on one side. It was a long, awkward walk back to Aspen Hall, and I was looking forward to putting the night's events behind me.

We eventually got Ruby into her bed and I saw Jonah to our door. "Thanks for your help."

"Of course," he replied. "It was my pleasure." He put his hands in his pockets and shifted his weight nervously, leaning against the doorway. "How much..." He trailed off, cheeks flushed red, and motioned to Ruby, who had already fallen asleep in a lump atop her mattress, with her mouth hanging open. "How much of *us* did you see?"

"More than I'd have liked to," I said coldly.

"Look, I'm really sorry," he said. "I feel terrible, I..."

"You don't have to apologize to me," I replied, trying to hide the fact that I wished he had been kissing me at that party, not Ruby.

"I just want you to know." He paused. "It was a mistake. I shouldn't have kissed her."

"It's fine," I said. "It's not like you need my approval to kiss my roommate." I looked down at my feet, kicking a loose tile on the floor.

He picked up my chin with one finger. "Do I need your approval to kiss you?" His voice was breathy, quiet.

I sucked in a breath, taken aback. My heart was thunderous in my chest. For once, I knew my answer. I didn't overthink a thing. I just gave him a warm smile and closed my eyes, leaning towards him. I was so ready to kiss him, I could almost hear the drumroll in my head…

"Ow," Ruby whined, sitting up in her bed and clutching her stomach.

Jonah and I instinctively pulled away from one another. I rushed to Ruby's bedside. "What do you need? Do you think you're gonna be sick?"

She nodded and I grabbed her trash can from under her bed and handed it to her.

"Thank you," I mouthed to Jonah. He gave me a curt nod and left my room, shutting the door behind him.

10

Lillian

Adagio, Maine, 1934

I stood on our front porch and read the note, thanking God that I had been the one to find it and not my parents.

It read:

Dear Lillian,

I sincerely apologize for the actions of my little brother. Times have been difficult for my family, and we've had to turn to any means possible for food and shelter. Please know that my brother meant no harm in his escapades. I can assure you, Timothy is just a hungry boy, not a criminal. He had chosen your garden by mere coincidence. I promise you, he hadn't any idea that we've met. I hope you'll look past his mistakes and not report him to the authorities.

Yours truly,

Henry Quinn

I held the note close to me for a moment, then tucked it into the top of my dress, the only reasonable hiding place for something of this nature. I was having some difficulty wrapping my head around the fact that the boy I had seen was Henry's younger brother. I had even more trouble coming to terms with the fact that he was struggling so badly. *If only I had known when we first met,* I thought, *I'd have made sure to give him something more than just medical care.* My heart sank as I remembered what tough times we were going through, knowing that my family was doing just fine, our lavish estate and extra cash keeping us warm and fed. Others, I knew, were not so lucky. Henry was of the latter category.

As I headed back inside, I thought up a plan for how I could see him again, partly because I wanted to tell him that I knew the loss of a few of our tomatoes wasn't his fault, and, well... Just because I wanted to see him again.

A few days later, after some extensive contemplation, I decided I could go back to the pub where I first met Henry, given that the owner would let us both in again, after the events of the previous week. Father had left for business the day before and wouldn't be back for at least three days. That gave me ample time to go find Henry.

The door to the pub swung open in a single, swift motion. I entered, saying a silent prayer that the owner would be kind, and that I'd hear the sweet sounds of Henry's piano playing as I entered.

Unfortunately, neither wish came true.

"Miss Abbott," I heard his voice boom the second he recognized me. "Have you learned nothing from our last encounter?"

"I'm very sorry, Sir," I said, trying to keep my cool and not sound as nervous as I truly was. "I was just wondering if you could tell me where your pianist is."

The man shrugged. "He hasn't been back since you were here."

"Could you tell me where he lives?" I asked, not daring to move an inch closer to the man, his daunting glare still etched clearly in my memory.

"Not sure," he said. "The chap's dirt poor, though. He probably lives over on Sixth Avenue." He paused. "That's what you get for trying to be a musician during these times instead of trying to get a real job."

I chose to ignore the anger burning inside of me at his last statement. My heart felt suddenly heavy, burdened with the knowledge of Henry's living situation. I wished there was something I could do to ease his struggle.

Something deep inside told me I had to, though. So I did. "Thank you," I said to the owner, who was busy wiping down his bar.

He gave me a nod. "Good day, Miss." I took his hint and rushed out of the pub, immediately heading west, towards Sixth Avenue.

I could smell it before I could see it, and my heart ached for everyone who had to spend their days there. Walking slowly into the row of little shacks and sheds, I couldn't help but wish there was something I could do to make things better. Under my breath, I cursed my father for keeping his fortune all to himself.

Sixth Avenue was small – just a single block of tiny houses crammed with way too many people. It was Adagio's own little Hooverville, and it made me absolutely sick.

My stomach churned as I trudged deeper into the abyss of poverty. I was starting to regret my journey, seeing rows of these tiny disasters of homes on either side of me, people sitting in the ground with nowhere to go. I kept my eyes peeled for Henry or his brother. In the distance, I could hear the soft sound of a songbird and took a deep breath, reminded that even in the worst of places, beauty can be found.

"Lillian?"

His voice came from behind me and I immediately turned around. "Henry!" I said.

"What are you doing here?" He approached me at a brisk walk, grabbing my hands in his.

"I just, I... I had to tell you about the tomatoes."

He let out a quiet chuckle. "What?"

"The tomatoes," I repeated. "The ones your brother stole. I let him take them."

Henry shook his head and sighed, smiling. "You're too generous for your own good, Lillian Abbott." He paused. "Thank you."

"It was nothing, really," I said. "I'm so sorry I didn't do more, if only I had known, I..." I trailed off when Henry dropped my hands and turned away from me. "What's the matter?"

"I think you should go," he told me.

"What?"

"You don't belong here," he said. He turned back around and looked into my eyes. "I don't want to pull you down into this mess."

"You're not pulling me down." My brow furrowed in confusion. I just wanted him to let me help him. I looked around, suddenly remembering our surroundings. "Can we go somewhere and talk?"

He nodded once and led me down the block to a single bench shaded by trees just a few feet past Sixth Avenue. "What is it?" he asked, gesturing for me to sit.

"I don't understand," I said. "You don't want me to be a part of your life?"

"No, no, it's not that at all," he responded quickly, sitting down beside me. "I would love to get to know you. You've been incredibly kind to me. However…" he trailed off, looking away.

"What is it?" I rested my hand on his.

He remained silent for a moment. "I'm not successful, Lillian. I can't provide for anyone. I can't even care for my own brother."

"So? What does that matter?"

"It means I'll never be great. I'll never be wealthy enough to even consider courting someone like you."

I looked into his eyes, sadness creeping into them. "What are you saying?"

He took my hands. "I have a sinking feeling it means your family will never approve of me," he said frankly.

The rest of the conversation was just as unpleasant. I regretted ever taking the trip to Sixth Avenue. What was I thinking? I knew I'd never have a chance with Henry. Circumstances were too difficult; my father's standards were too high.

Too high, I thought to myself again, a dark amusement tickling my senses. I wondered how someone as sweet and caring as Henry could ever fall below someone's standards. But that was Father.

I arrived back at home after about fifteen minutes of walking, and collapsed into my bed, alone to think about my missed chance at romance.

"Lillian!" my mother called. My peace was interrupted after just a few short moments.

I went downstairs to see what was the matter. My father stood in the doorway. "Father," I said, feigning cheerfulness. "You're home early. What a pleasant surprise!"

"And look who he brought home!" Mother exclaimed.

I gave my father a questioning look and he stepped aside, allowing a young man to walk in the door behind him. "This is Paul," Father said. "I think you two will get along just perfectly."

11

Charlie

Pine Ridge University, 1990

The day after the party, I awoke just in time for my class. Fearing I would be late, I gathered my things, threw my hair into a messy bun, and went to class in a casual jeans and t-shirt combo. I sat in my Literature class for about an hour, listening to old Dr. Wells drone on and on about symbolism in Shakespeare's greatest works. If I'd had time for coffee that morning, I may have been slightly more interested in the material.

I sent a silent *thank you!* to God when the class was finally over and I could head into the music building to grab a coffee and get ready for my first orchestra practice. The one person I did *not* expect to see in a formal orchestra setting was the one person I saw, along with his right-hand bandmate.

"You play the cello?"

"No," Jonah said with a laugh. "But I need an orchestra credit for my degree, so here we are."

"Same," Shane interjected, brandishing a beautiful baroque-style viola. "We're giving it our best shot."

I laughed and took a sip of my coffee. "You two are ridiculous."

"We know," Shane said. He left us, heading in the conductor's direction, probably to ask where violas are meant to sit.

Jonah took a small step closer to me. "About last night..." He began quietly.

"I forgive you." I cleared my throat, more than ready to be finished with the subject. "Let's just forget the whole thing." I didn't give him time to answer before walking off to my seat, beside a rather beautiful redheaded violin player. "Hi," I said to her, sitting down and pulling my violin out of its case.

"Hey," she answered. "I'm Emily."

"My name's Charlie. Are you a music major?"

"Music performance, yes," she said, as she began some warm-up scales.

Jonah sat down behind me, and Shane was on the other side of the arc. "There are two boys in this orchestra who have never touched classical instruments," I said to her, a playful smirk on my face.

"What?" Emily laughed. "I wonder how long it's gonna take for Dr. Grey to kick them out!"

It didn't take very long. We were only halfway through our first rendition of Vivaldi's *The Four Seasons* when the conductor, Dr. Grey, stopped everything and stared Shane down. "Hey, Blondie," he snapped.

"Yes, Sir," Shane looked up from his sheet music.

"Where did you learn to play the viola?"

"I didn't, Sir," he replied.

"Quit calling me that," said Dr. Grey. "And get your ass out of here until you learn how to play the viola!"

Emily and I exchanged looks and tried to hold in our invasive laughter. "So, you know him, I take it?" she whispered.

"Yeah, you could say that," I responded, giggling.

Jonah did a better job of blending in, but by the halfway point of the rehearsal, his cover was blown. "You there, with the cello," called out Dr. Grey.

"Hmm?"

"Are you pals with that other bloke?"

"What other bloke?"

"Oh, shut up and go learn the cello!" Dr. Grey furrowed his brow and stroked his beard in frustration. As Jonah stood up to leave, he continued. "Does anyone else here *not* know how to play an instrument? I thought I was doing you folks a favor by not requiring auditions for this ensemble, but maybe I was mistaken."

We all nodded our heads in false solemnity, holding back laughter as we watched Jonah wade his way through the maze of chairs, music stands and instrument cases.

The rest of the rehearsal went slowly and simply. No more musicians were kicked out, and no one else made fatal errors halfway through Vivaldi's greatest works. "So, those musical imposters," Emily began as we started packing up at the end of rehearsal.

"What about them?"

"They're both pretty cute. You aren't... You know, dating either of them, are you?"

I let out a ridiculous laugh. "Not quite, no."

"You want to, though? I can tell." Emily closed the snaps on her violin case and stood up. "You can tell me, I don't bite."

"I mean, last night, I nearly kissed one of them." I stood up and slung my violin case over one shoulder, grabbing my half-finished coffee in my free hand.

"Ooh, juicy!" She followed close behind me as we exited the rehearsal hall.

"He actually kissed my roommate, though," I said.

Emily stopped dead in her tracks. "No, he didn't!"

I nodded. "He did. But he felt terrible. He told me he'd have rather kissed me."

She shook her head in denial. "No, nope, absolutely not. Kick him to the curb, Sweetheart."

"Really? He's so nice, and he apologized so much, and I was totally ready to kiss him. Like, I leaned in."

"You didn't!" Emily's voice grew more intense with each sentence.

"I did," I replied, turning towards the exit.

She clicked her tongue and shook her head. "Don't let him fool you," Emily said. "He sounds like bad news."

"How? He apologized."

"He seems apologetic now, but just wait until he *does* kiss you, then says that was a mistake too!" She gave me an inquisitive look. "Didn't you say you wanted to focus more on classes anyway?"

"Well, yes," I conceded.

"Best thing to do is forget about him, then," Emily warned as we parted ways.

I pondered what she had said for a few moments as I walked back to my dorm. What if Emily was right? What if Jonah did just want to kiss me, and nothing more? What if he wasn't all that nice, after all?

I tried to rid myself of those worrying thoughts as I entered the elevator and hit the fourth-floor button. *Jonah's in the past,* I told myself. *He was yesterday's problem. Stop worrying about what he thinks and move on. Focus on the present. On the important.*

The elevator stopped on the second floor. "Well, hello there," a boy's voice echoed through the elevator chamber as he joined me.

"Hi," I said.

We stood there in silence for a few moments. "I have to say it," he said, scratching his head through finely trimmed dirty-blond hair.

"Hmm?"

"You're so beautiful."

"Oh." I blushed. "Thank you." I looked down at my shoes, taking a loose strand of hair and tucking it behind my ear.

"Would you want to get lunch together tomorrow at noon in the cafeteria?"

He's... Direct, I thought to myself. Still, I was looking for a way to stop thinking about Jonah. Maybe this was the answer. "Sure," I replied. "I'm Charlie, by the way."

"My name's Mike. I'll see you tomorrow." He winked at me and we both exited the elevator, turning in opposite directions.

"Charlie!" Ruby exclaimed as I entered the room. "You're just the person I wanted to see."

"That's great, Rubes, because I live here," I said with a sarcastic grin.

"Oh, shut up." She laughed, tossing a pillow in my direction. "Look, I need you to help me piece together last night."

I caught the pillow before it smacked me in the face. "Nothing really happened," I explained. "You got absolutely wasted, so Jonah helped me get you back here, then you threw up a few times and went to bed."

She made a *humph* sound and shrugged. "Alrighty, then," she said, hopping to the floor and taking the pillow from my hands. "I was hoping it had been a little more exciting." She tossed the pillow back onto the bed.

"I mean, you kissed Jonah," I said, after a brief internal argument over whether or not I should have withheld that little detail. "Two guys got into a fight, nearly smashed a bench, but that was just about all the excitement we had after the little concert in the common room."

Ruby's jaw dropped and she whirled around to face me. "I kissed *him*? He's *so* attractive, I can't believe I actually got him to kiss me! Does he like me? He's single, right?"

I rolled my eyes. "I don't know," I said. "Maybe you should talk to him." *Don't say anything to him,* I wanted to tell her, *I have a huge crush on him!*

"I think I will," she said, gathering a jacket and her backpack. "Okay, then. I'm gonna go to the library to do a little bit of homework. Wanna come?"

"Um, no, I think I'm gonna stay back this time. Thanks, though."

"Sure."

The door clicked behind her and I collapsed into my bed. *Stop overthinking everything and do your homework!* I thought to myself as I let out an exasperated sigh.

Soon, I would meet Mike for lunch. He'd teach me to stop worrying about boys who kiss girls' roommates, and then I could put it all behind me. I could move on and *stop* worrying about boys altogether…

I scowled at myself. The plan only sounded worse the more I thought about it. *A distraction from being distracted*, I thought, trying to piece it together for myself, *so I won't be distracted anymore?*

I groaned, rolling over and hiding my face in my pillows, trying to clear my head of everything that had happened. I groaned even louder when I realized that I couldn't truly succeed in my efforts to clear my head when Jonah seemed to plague my every thought.

12

Lillian

Adagio, Maine, 1934

"Hello, Paul," I said to the tall, redheaded man standing in the doorway.

"Good evening, Lillian." He entered and planted a firm kiss on the back of my hand, the wiry hairs of his scruffy, unkempt beard itching my skin. "Your father has told me so much about you!"

"All good things, I hope," I said with a forced chuckle.

"Oh, yes, he told me you are just an outstanding young woman," Paul said enthusiastically. "I hope you'll accept this." He held out a single red rose and gave a slight bow.

I cringed a little on the inside at his awkwardly executed romantic gesture, but accepted the rose, not wanting to embarrass him in front of my parents. "Thank you." I took the flower in both hands, sniffing it for added effect. "It's beautiful."

"I'll fetch some water and a vase," my mother said, and hurried away.

"I thought you two would truly make a great pair." I jumped at the sound of my father's voice from behind me. "I've arranged for you to get dinner this evening at Lillian's favorite restaurant in town."

"Your father is quite a remarkable man," Paul said to me. "You don't know how lucky you are to have grown up in such a household."

If only you knew, Paul, I thought. "Yes, I'm very lucky," I conceded.

My mother returned and gave me a kiss on the forehead. "Have a lovely time tonight," she said.

"I will, Mother," I replied, pulling her in for a hug.

"Alright, then, off you go." She smiled and gave me a pat on the back.

Paul and I walked side by side, with Father a few paces ahead. He started up his expensive Chevrolet and

Paul opened the back door for me. "Thank you," I said, climbing in.

My date and I sat in the back of the car while Father acted as chauffeur. Paul held my hand in his and smiled at me. I feigned a smile in return, trying to figure out when would be the best time to tell him that I was pointlessly hung up on an impoverished musician from Sixth Avenue.

When we arrived at the restaurant, a quaint family-run kitchen called Harrington's. My childhood best friend, Elizabeth, was the owner's daughter. On occasion, Ben and I would visit the restaurant to check on the Harrington family, just to see how they were doing. We would stay for lunch and Elizabeth and I would try to catch up, but after years of being involved in two very different lives, we had grown apart. She worked tirelessly every day with her mother in the kitchen, trying to keep their business afloat, and I spent my days begging my father to let me leave our pointlessly large house.

"You two have a fantastic time," my father said, an artificial note of cheerfulness in his voice. "I'll come back to pick you up in two hours."

We thanked him and headed into the restaurant. We sat in silence for a few moments, neither one of us quite sure of what to say. "So…" I finally ventured, "You work with my father?"

"Well, I work *for* him, actually," Paul replied. "He hired me a few weeks ago as his assistant. A real saving grace, your father is."

"Oh, yes. I'm glad." I opened my menu and started to browse, despite having memorized its contents years ago.

"I wish I was as lucky as you are," he said again.

I didn't have a reply. I didn't want to judge Paul, I truly didn't. But something about him was really starting to bother me.

He continued. "You have a wonderful house, lots of money, four amazing siblings, and two absolutely lovely parents. I'd give anything for something like that."

Okay, I understand. You have a difficult life. Leave mine alone. "Oh? What was your childhood like, Paul?"

He absentmindedly fiddled with his napkin. "Oh, I grew up in a mansion about an hour from Portland…" He began, then trailed off. "It was nothing special. I wouldn't really care to discuss it."

"That's okay," I responded, trying to think of another conversation topic while wondering why a boy who grew up in a mansion was now working as an assistant. I also wondered why Father had planned for me to dine with someone who was beneath him on the economic ladder.

"Lily, how are you doing?" I looked up to see Elizabeth standing by our table.

"Pretty good," I said to my childhood friend. "How are you?"

"I've been great," she responded. "Just got engaged!"

I took a close look at the simple ring on her finger. "It's beautiful," I told her. "Who's the lucky man?"

"His name is Alfred. My father introduced us, he's so wonderful." Paul gave me a look. Elizabeth cleared her throat. "Anyway," she continued, "What would you two like to order?"

When Elizabeth finished taking our orders, I was eager to move the subject past her recent engagement, hoping Paul wouldn't get any ideas. "Are you going to school for anything?"

"Oh, no," he said. "I'm not nearly wealthy enough for formal schooling. I'm just so grateful your father has given me a stable job working with him."

The rest of our date was much of the same. I tried to keep conversations light as I slowly ate a small bowl of soup, but nothing worked. Every other sentence Paul spoke was an inspired praise of my father. My stomach began to hurt when I thought of Paul becoming part of our family. I couldn't finish my soup.

When the date was finally over, Paul paid the bill, despite how poor he told me he was. I'd have considered it a friendly gesture if I hadn't been so angered at his earlier actions.

"Thank you," I told him as he held the door for us to leave. My father hadn't yet arrived to drive us back home, so we decided to go for a walk around the block.

"No," Paul said, "Thank you. Thank you for giving me a chance tonight." He took my hand and we began to walk down the street, watching the sun slowly set past the simple Adagio skyline.

"Of course," I replied. "It was very nice meeting you." It wasn't a complete lie – was it?

Paul stopped and turned to me. "You're a lovely woman," he said.

"Well, thank you." Despite my distaste for him, I found myself blushing.

"Do you... Do you think you'd like to see me again?"

I thought about it for a moment. All in all, Paul wasn't all bad, and clearly Father actually approved of him, unlike one particular green-eyed piano player. I looked up at him, only just then noticing that he was nearly a whole foot taller than I, and nodded. "Yes," I said, trying not to sound resigned. "It's just…"

"You're pining for someone else," Paul said knowingly.

"What?"

"I can see it in your eyes," he continued. He took my hands in his and continued. "There's someone else out there you're thinking about."

Tears started burning in my eyes. I fought them back with everything I had. "Paul, I…"

"Look," he said. "I know that I'll never be perfect. I'll never be that man who you've been dreaming about. I'll never be your everything. But I think… I think I can be *something* to you. If you just give me a chance."

I nodded, reminded of the resounding "no" I had received from Henry just hours before. "Yes," I said. "My father is hosting a house party this Saturday for his business acquaintances, I'm sure he's told you. Why don't you accompany me?"

"That sounds perfect," he responded, pulling me in for a hug.

13

Charlie

Pine Ridge University, 1990

It was Friday, the last day of my first week of classes. My morning classes bored me, as usual, and in Music Theory I made sure to sit as far away from Jonah and his friends as I could. If I was going to get over my little crush, I had to put as much distance between us as possible.

Once I finished with classes, I headed to the cafeteria to meet Mike for lunch. I saw him sitting at a table when I got there, and he waved to get my attention. "Hey," I said, taking a seat beside him.

"Hey," he replied. "Wanna go get some food?"

I smiled and nodded, and the two of us walked up to the buffet line together. After getting a modest portion of sushi and rice, I returned to our little table. I bit my lip nervously, not sure of what Mike was thinking. He made some small talk with me and my nerves started to calm.

"What's your major?" He asked me, taking a huge bite of a burger.

"Music education," I said. I played with a loose strand of hair. "What's yours?"

"Business management," Mike replied. "Music, huh? I'll bet you're really talented, then."

I could feel myself blushing, so I took a sip of water in the hopes that he wouldn't notice. "Um, I guess you could say that," I said with a forced laugh.

"Charlie!"

A chill ran down my spine as I heard his voice projecting from behind me. I didn't turn around to acknowledge it. I had spent the entire day doing everything I could to avoid Jonah, and I planned to continue.

"Who's that?" Mike asked me, leaning to see who had arrived at the dining hall.

I sunk down into my seat, hiding my face. "His name is Jonah," I said.

"What does he want with you?" asked Mike. "I was expecting we'd have this lunch to ourselves."

"I'm sorry," I replied, embarrassed. "He's a friend, I think. It's a long story."

"Does he have feelings for you?"

Taken aback by his brash statement, I replied, "I don't know. I've only known him a few days. What does it matter?"

"Well, I'm going to be honest with you," said Mike, "I came on this date thinking I would be able to win your heart, but it clearly lies elsewhere."

"What? My heart does not-"

"You're really bad at hiding it," Mike explained.

Jonah arrived at our table. "Charlie!" he said again, "I didn't see you in Theory today. Is everything al-" noticing Mike, he stopped. "Who's this?"

"This is Mike," I said.

"Hi there, Mike." Jonah put one hand on the table and one on Mike's shoulder. "Could I have a word with Charlie, please?"

"Sure, whatever," Mike said through clenched teeth. "Charlie, I'll be in the lobby when you're done." He tossed down his napkin and headed out of the cafeteria. I fidgeted, suddenly feeling guilty for having caused so much grief.

Jonah took Mike's seat once he was gone and I huffed. "What do you want, Jonah?"

He flinched, apparently surprised at my attitude, as if I didn't have a right to be frustrated with him. "I just wanted to let you know that Shane and I signed you up to be our third group member for that Music Theory project." He paused, noticing my expression. "Are you upset with me?"

"You kissed my roommate," I said. "And then you tried to kiss me."

"You didn't argue with me," he countered.

"I had alcohol in my system!"

"You took *one* sip of vodka!"

I let out a sigh of exasperation. "What does it matter? It's over now. I've moved on, Jonah."

"To what? To Mike?" Jonah gestured towards the door.

"Yes, to Mike!" I said in a quiet, fierce voice. "Is there something wrong with that? He's kind, gentle…"

"You don't even know him," he said, rolling his eyes.

I glared at him, the heat between us quickly becoming too much to ignore. After a moment, I looked away and said, "I don't know you, either."

"Really?" He asked. Without giving me a chance to answer, he went on, speaking quickly, jaw clenched. "Okay. You want to know me?"

"I-"

"Well, I've been playing the bass for six years. My favorite color is red. I have a younger sister and two dogs. I wear this old bandana all the time because I'm insecure about my hairline," he said, pulling it off his head and slamming it on the table. "I'm way too into Bon Jovi and I wish I never would've kissed your roommate, because I'm so damn into *you*!" He stopped for a moment, glancing about the room and lowering his voice. "If that's your only excuse for not being with me, then maybe I was wrong about you." He stood up, tied his bandana back on his head, and walked off.

Stunned, I sat alone for a moment, staring into my sushi and wishing I knew what to do. *Kick him to the curb,* I remembered Emily saying. Should I listen to her sensibility? Or should I give in to Jonah, to his unwavering persistence, to the warm sensation I had whenever he came near me?

I thought about it for a few moments before leaving the dining hall. I had already planned to try to move on from Jonah. It wasn't fair. He went after Ruby first, not me. I wasn't going to let his little outburst get in the way of my plans to move on. I chose not to change my mind yet again and went back to see the man I was trying so hard to distract myself with.

Ugh, what am I doing?

"Hi, Mike," I said warily, sitting down with him in the lobby just outside the dining hall. "I'm… uh, I'm so sorry about that."

"I'm sorry, too," he said. "I overreacted. I shouldn't have snapped like I did. We barely know each other; you're entitled to being friends with whoever you choose. I'm sure that guy just had something simple to ask you about, and it's not my place to be concerned in your affairs."

"Thank you for understanding," I said.

Mike nodded. "Anyway, where were we?" He clicked his tongue a few times, thinking. "Oh right," he continued. "Your brilliant music career."

I laughed. "I'm not exactly in it for the fame and glory," I said. "Are you into music at all?"

He guffawed, as if the idea was preposterous. "Absolutely not." When he saw my critical expression, he elaborated. "Not that it isn't incredible," he continued. "It's just something I would never really choose to do. I don't find it…" he searched for the right word. "Satisfying."

"Oh."

"I don't mean to offend you," he continued. "I'm just trying to be honest."

"I get that. Thanks." I shifted in my seat, trying to find some common ground with Mike. "Why did you choose to come here for college?" I asked, hoping that maybe he, too, was here on a scholarship as a first-generation student.

"I'm a legacy," he said. *So much for that.* "My dad came here back in the seventies, and his dad before him. I never even had to make a choice about college, I was born into a Pine Ridge family."

"That's great," I said.

A guy who looked at least two years older than us approached Mike. "You still coming?" he asked in a hushed voice.

Mike nodded, glancing my way. "Girls still get in free?"

The mysterious upperclassman responded, "Yeah," then looked at me and winked. I was dressed modestly, but something about his wandering eyes made me feel somewhat violated.

As he walked off, Mike inched closer to me. "How do you feel about going to an absolutely radical party with me? It's at the end of the month. Pi Kappa Phi hosts a legendary banger at the end of September every year."

"I mean, I'm not really the partying type," I said honestly.

"Oh, come on, I'll be right there with you," he said. "If you don't like it, we can go somewhere else. It's on a Friday!" He elbowed me, very enthusiastic about what was clearly his favorite day of the week.

"Okay, I guess it can't hurt," I replied. I knew I would grow to regret the decision, but going to a party with Mike seemed like the perfect chance for me to prove to both Jonah and myself that I had moved on. Plus, once Mike would inevitably realize we weren't compatible, we would break up and I could go back to focusing on school, just like my mom had asked me to on the very day she and Dad dropped me off.

I sat there for a few more awkward moments, looking at Mike, praying my plan would work, cursing myself for getting involved in such a mess so early in the semester.

14

Lillian

Adagio, Maine, 1934

I clasped the final button on my lavender-colored evening dress and smoothed down my unruly blonde hair. I took a deep breath, telling myself that tonight would be a success, and willing myself to focus on starting a good, healthy relationship with Paul. Music was already filling the house, and mindless chatter had begun in accompaniment. Knowing Paul would arrive any minute, I headed down the staircase to join my siblings and wait for my date.

"Well, look at you," said Ben, "Lovely, as always."

"And you're looking dapper as ever," I replied, gesturing to his bowtie. "Have you seen Mary and Robert?"

“I think they’re raiding the kitchen,” Ben replied. “Trying to get to the hors d’oeuvres before Father’s guests do.”

While laughing with my brother, I noticed a familiar redhead out of the corner of my eye and headed to the doorway to greet him. “Good evening, Paul,” I said, and led him to where my brother was standing. “Ben, this is Paul.”

Ben shot me a confused look while shaking Paul’s hand. He always was able to read my mind like it was a good book. “Paul,” he said anyway, “I hope you have a wonderful time at our father’s gala.”

“I’m sure I will,” he replied. “I’ve got great company.” He offered his arm and we headed deeper into the foyer, taking seats near the entrance to the parlor, where someone I had never seen before played a mediocre melody on our family piano.

“Thank you for coming,” I said to him. “It means a lot to me.”

“It’s my pleasure, truly,” replied Paul. “I’m glad you decided to give me a chance.”

“I am, too.” Even I was shocked to hear such a blatant lie leave my lips.

"Attention, everyone." My father's shoes clicked against the tile flooring as he strutted to the center of the foyer. The crowd hushed, and the music stopped. "Thank you all for coming," he said. "I've brought us all together this evening to bask in the glory of fellowship and to simply enjoy each other's company." He lifted his half-full glass of expensive chardonnay. I wondered who he had to swindle in order to get his hands on such a drink. "Here's to a memorable night!"

Gleeful choruses of "here, here!" filled the foyer.

The group of guests slowly meandered into the parlor, where my mother served them her homemade finger sandwiches and the pianist resumed his melody. I tried to relax and have a good time, but I feared I would be eternally guarded at my father's social events, despite knowing he'd never lay a hand on me while his colleagues were present, for fear he'd slander his own reputation.

"Would you care to dance?" Paul offered his hand.

I accepted, and we moved to the center of the room in one swift, fleeting motion. Father had made sure I had received proper lessons in dance at a very young age, although I remembered having fierce arguments with him about them. "I don't need to learn to dance!" I would shout. "I only want to do things I enjoy!"

"Then maybe you should learn to enjoy it," he would reply through gritted teeth, pushing me into the parlor where I would meet my instructor.

In this moment, though, I had made the decision on my own, the decision to let Paul wrap his arm around my waist and lead me in a traditional waltz. Still, as our feet maneuvered gracefully across the floor, I couldn't help but wonder if Father had made sure his assistant, his little puppet known as Paul, had studied up on his dancing before coming to the gala. I did all I could to stop thinking of Paul in such a negative manner, but every time I thought I'd moved past it, those thoughts would come creeping right back.

"Your earrings are spectacular," Paul said.

"Thank you." I lifted a hand and brushed my finger against one of the silver hoops. "They were a gift from my mother."

"You live such a beautiful, fortunate life," he said, as I tried not to roll my eyes. He twirled me and dipped me with one sturdy arm. "I'm so grateful you've allowed me to be a part of it."

I was starting to regret that decision, but there was no way I could tell him that in the middle of the party. I didn't know what I wanted from him. Was I seeking closure from my misfortune with Henry? Was I trying, for once, to gain my father's approval? Did I just want to have someone, *anyone*? I thought it best to end things. I didn't want to start a relationship with this kind of dishonesty.

"I know," I said to him, avoiding eye contact. "Could we go talk somewhere alone?"

He nodded. "Is something the matter? Have I done something?"

"No, you've done nothing wrong." I glanced around the room, all too aware of the nervous beating of my heart. "I just… Need to be alone with you."

"Of course. After you."

I led him out of the parlor and around our large staircase, toward the front porch. "Here," I said, gesturing to the two-seated swing that Father and Ben had installed just a few weeks prior. "Sit." I paused for a moment, conjuring up the courage to tell him what I was thinking.

"Could I say something?" Paul asked, his jarring words interrupting my thoughts.

I simply nodded.

"I admire you, Lillian," he said. He stood up and began pacing slowly, wandering about the porch. Everything I've learned about you, from your father, from our few moments together… It's been amazing, and I…"

I followed, meeting him at the top of the porch stairs, the same stairs I had run down when I stormed out of the house just two short weeks before. “Paul, please-”

He continued, disregarding my plea to speak. “May I kiss you?”

I was instantly taken aback by his request. I had only met him a few days prior, did he really think I was so irresistible? I was trying to tell him that I didn’t think we were right for each other, but he was just so insistent. “I…”

He didn’t let me finish my thought, interrupting me by quickly pulling me against him and planting a fat, juicy kiss right on my lips. A chill ran up my spine and my blood went cold. His beard scratched my face and I pushed him away. “I’m sorry, Paul. I…”

He took a step back and scratched the back of his neck. “No, I’m sorry. Are you alright? I don’t know what came over me, I just-”

“No, no, it’s okay,” I said, trying my best to regain my composure. “You’re fine. It’s me. I was surprised, is all.” I paused. “But, Paul, listen. I don’t think we should see each other anymore.”

“Oh,” he said, turning away from me. “But we… We had planned to try. You said-”

"Paul, I have tried. But you know I wasn't sure about… about *us* from the start." I looked away from him, worried I would start to cry. "It just… It's not right."

He exhaled slowly. I couldn't figure out if he was frustrated or resigned. "I thought…" he said. "I thought you decided I deserved a chance."

"I did!" I said. "I mean, you do. Just… Not with me." I took his hand. "It's not that you don't deserve to be happy," I added. "I just don't think *I'm* your happiness."

"What are you saying?"

"I'm saying that I think you're a great person, Paul, I really do. But I also think that you work for my father, and I think he convinced you to come home and meet me by talking about me as if I'm some perfect person with a perfect life. I'm not who you think I am."

"Lillian," he said. "Everything I've learned about you is absolutely beautiful. You don't have to be in love with me. I respect that, I respect *you.*"

"Thank you for that," I replied, silently wondering how this man was just a perfect example of a human contradiction.

"Goodbye, Lillian," Paul said, dropping my hands and starting down the staircase.

"Goodbye, Paul." I sat on the top stair, teary-eyed, and watched him leave, waving as he faded from view.

In the distance, I thought I could see Henry's silhouette, the moonlight dancing across his slender figure. I stood up and turned away, pained by the thought. I decided that my mind was playing tricks on me, and went back inside, through the large clusters of people, and to my bed.

15

Charlie

A random frat house, Pine Ridge University, 1990

We arrived at the house at around ten on the night of the party. My heart pounded as we approached the door, suddenly reminded of my last experience at one of these events. "Ready?"

"Yes," I responded to Mike, and he wrapped his arm around me, his hand resting at the small of my back. We walked in, and I was expecting a scene similar to what I had witnessed at the party at the suites on Monday. What we encountered, though, was somehow much worse.

"This is awesome!" shouted Mike over deathly loud music. The room was completely dark aside from the occasional flashes of colored light from someone's makeshift disco ball. There has hardly room to move, let alone breathe, and every few seconds another weird frat guy ended up crowd surfing. None of that surprised me too much, though.

"Live music!" Mike gestured to the front of the room, where a platform-style stage sat perpendicular to the door. On it stood five boys in grey t-shirts – one singing, two on guitar, one on drums, and one bass player with a green bandana that I knew all too well. I could feel myself almost being pulled in his direction.

No, I reminded myself. I could *not* fall into that trap. I had to listen to my head and ignore the ever-quickening beat of my heart.

I whipped my head around to face away from the stage, praying Jonah wouldn't see me. I had been too embarrassed to face him one-on-one since his little outburst at lunch a few weeks prior. Despite Shane having signed us up to be in the same group for a huge project, I had managed to keep our contact minimal, and I was starting to think he understood that I wasn't interested in dating him. As soon as I was certain Jonah had given up trying, I could break up with Mike and be done worrying about boys for good. I could start to focus on the things that really mattered.

That is, if I could ever actually get him out of my head.

"Wanna get something to drink?" Mike asked me.

"Yes, please," I said. I knew there was no chance I'd survive the night if I had to do it sober.

He took my hand and led me down a hallway where all the drinks I could've imagined sat on a flimsy plastic table. Mike poured a shot of some clear liquid and handed it to me. "Have you ever done this before?"

I shook my head.

"Swallow it fast," he said. "It's gonna burn."

I closed my eyes and clenched my left fist, taking the drink in my right. He was right, it burned like hell. "Holy *shit*!" I screamed, once I finished.

Mike laughed and took three right in a row. "Isn't it great?" He asked.

My muscles were already starting to feel looser, and I was no longer regretting my decision to go to the party that night. "It's awesome!" I replied. "Can I have another?"

He gave me another shot and I downed it faster than the first. We wandered away from the drinks and ended up on the dance floor, both of us becoming a part of the mess of writhing bodies jiving awkwardly to the music. I wasn't even worried about Jonah seeing me anymore. Mike and I were pressed up against each other, his hands moving about my body as we danced.

I had two more shots by the time midnight came. I felt like a new me. I didn't overthink anything anymore, I wasn't constantly worried about school and my scholarship and Jonah and Mike. All I had to worry about was myself, and how awesome this night was turning out.

"Charlie!" I tried to turn towards the sound, not sure where it had come from. "Charlie, over here!" Eventually, I found Mike making his way towards me. My legs were getting tired from bouncing.

"Mike!" I threw my arms around him. "Hey."

"Hi, Charlie," he said. "I thought I lost you for a minute there."

"Nope," I told him. "I'm still right here."

"Attention, lovely people of Pi Kappa Phi!"

We turned our attention to the stage, where Cedar was yelling a bit too enthusiastically into the microphone. "Ladies and gentlemen, we would like to turn the mic over to the one and only president of this bloody brilliant organization, Connor Hayes!" He was starting to sound like a bad sportscaster.

The house erupted with cheers as the guy Mike and I had seen earlier took the stage. He wore a blue collared shirt and a tie wrapped around his head. A strand of what looked like really old Mardi Gras beads rested on his neck. "Let's give a round of applause for our radical entertainers," he said, "For Madeleine!"

They continued to clap. I stopped, but I couldn't wipe the smile from my face. The little voice in my head that had been reminding me to be a good student and ignore my human instincts was quieting. My eyes wandered from the frat guy at the microphone to Jonah, standing towards the back of the stage, his mind clearly elsewhere. I bit my lip and thought about what it would be like if he kissed me.

"Alright, guys, okay!" Connor yelled. His voice pierced through the crowd's shenanigans. "Thank you all for coming to this event. I hope you've all been having a great night. I'm sure it's only gonna get better!" He raised up his red plastic cup and started screaming into the mic, which Cedar quickly pried from his hands.

"Okay," he said. "Does anyone else have anything to say?"

My hand shot up into the air before I knew what I was doing. "Me!" I yelled, working my way through the masses of people. I climbed up onto the stage and took the microphone in both of my hands. “Good evening, people,” I said quietly, trying my best to speak clearly.

“Get it over with!” A random voice shouted from the crowd.

“You got it!” I yelled back, flipping him off. A slow, increasingly loud “whoa” echoed across the crowd. “Okay,” I started up again. “My name is Charlotte Quinn. I’m dating that hunk of meat over there,” I hollered, pointing to Mike. The crowd cheered and Mike flexed his brawny arms. I turned towards the back of the stage, nearly tripping over the microphone wire as I caught Jonah’s eyes. My voice lowered. “But I wish I was dating that one.” I pointed right at him.

Jonah stood up and put his bass down, slowly starting towards me.

“He was a real asshole for a little bit,” I said. “But just look at that face.” My tongue was starting to feel like it didn’t belong in my mouth anymore, and I stumbled over my words. I did my best to hold back a huge, unruly burp.

“You really think that?” The microphone barely caught his words, but I could hear them loud and clear.

I nodded. “Mhm.” I fixed my eyes on him as he moved even closer. I couldn’t help but imagine the feeling of his hands in my hair, my arms around his waist, his lips on my lips.

I dropped the microphone to the ground as he closed the gap between us, readier than ever for him to kiss me. I closed my eyes and leaned into him, for the second time.

And I was interrupted. For the second time.

Mike flew onto the stage in one swift motion, planting his fist right on Jonah's nose. I darted back, suddenly snapping out of what felt almost like a trance. The crowd roared, some shouting, others chanting, a few voicing their concern. I stared at Mike, open-mouthed, not sure of what to say or do as the boys tussled, rolling across the stage.

Mike eventually stood, brushed himself off, and gave Jonah a menacing glare, as the bassist sat on the stage, wiping blood from his face as it dripped from his nose. "Don't. Kiss. My. Girlfriend!" He spat in Jonah's face, shoving him farther away from me with each word. When Jonah finally fell to the ground, Mike finished him off with a harsh kick to the gut, then grabbed me by the arm and led me out of the house. "Come on," he said to me, his voice gruff, "we're going home."

16

Lillian

Adagio, Maine, 1934

My hands shook as I held the note between my hands, reading it once, twice, a million times over.

Lovely Lillian,

I've written this letter time and again, hoping that I could find the words to express what I'm feeling, but it seems I am at a loss. The day you came to visit me at my home, I was upset. I was upset that you had to see me in that state, that you had come all that way just for me to tell you it wouldn't be worth it. I realized, later, that I was wrong, that it would have been worth every second, if I had only accepted your offer that day. And so, I wrote a letter at once, and I planned to drop it off at your home in person. I wrote that I had made a mistake, that I didn't want my fear of what could be to hold us back from something truly wonderful.

When I arrived, however, I saw that you had already moved on. I know now that you're better off without me. I'm sure that you will make that man very happy. He has no idea how lucky he is to have you by his side.

As I sit here writing this letter, my heart aches. I'm having trouble letting go of what I've lost. I can't seem to rid you from my mind. And so, I'll ask this of you: if you feel anything for me, anything at all, meet me at the docks tonight. I'll be waiting.

Sincerely yours,

Henry Quinn

I didn't know how many times I would have to read the letter before the message would sink in. I sat on the porch swing, holding the piece of paper close to me. I finally understood why I thought I had seen Henry that night. It was because I *had.*

A week had passed since Father's gala and my unnerving kiss with Paul. I had many regrets, but Paul was certainly my biggest. If I had never kissed him, if Henry had never seen us together...

But it didn't matter. It was over, and that night I would go to the docks. I would see him, and I would explain everything.

"Can you make sure Father and Mother are busy after supper?" I asked Ben later that same day.

He nodded. "I'll keep them occupied. Where are you going?"

"I'm meeting Henry by the docks," I replied.

A smile crept onto his face. "I knew it," he said. "I'm on your side, Lily. Always."

"Thank you," I replied, as grateful as ever that our bond had grown to the point of rule-breaking for each other's happiness.

"Stay safe," he said.

"Of course."

That night, when I finished helping my mother wash up after dinner, I executed my grand plan to sneak out and see Henry. I walked away from the kitchen, and into a hallway where there was a small alcove. From there, I took off my shoes in order to remain silent, treading lightly as I walked to the end of the hallway and out a side door. Shutting it quietly behind me, I said a silent prayer that Ben had managed to keep my parents far enough from our windows that they wouldn't see me sneaking through the front yard and to the street corner.

I could feel the cool ocean breeze on my skin and wrapped my shawl tighter against my body. I trudged on, confident that I would soon be able to clear the air with the man I couldn't stop thinking about.

A few minutes later, I finally reached the dock. The waves lapped calmly at its edge, where I could see Henry's silhouette shining in the moonlight just as it had been on that fateful night with Paul. He sat there all alone, tossing stones into the sea.

"Henry," I called to him.

He didn't hear. I broke into a jog.

"Henry," I called again.

The shaded figure at the edge of the dock rose and turned towards me. His eyes shone when he saw me running towards him "Lillian," he said, surprise filling his voice. "You came!" When he reached me, he pulled me into his arms in a warm, loving embrace.

"I came," I said. "I had to see you again."

"I'm so sorry for everything." He took my hands. "I let my fear get the better of me, I never should have turned you away like I did. I feel so strongly for you, Lillian. I just couldn't bear it any longer."

"I've thought of you every day."

"That man you were kissing-"

I interrupted him, needing to get the truth out as fast as possible. "My father had set us up. I didn't want to kiss him. It's over between us, now."

"You're sure?"

"Absolutely. We ended things."

"Lillian," Henry said nervously, running a hand through his thick, dark hair. "I don't want to ruin things. I don't want to stand in the way of your happiness."

"Don't you understand?" I asked him, bewildered by his statement. "Ever since we met, I can't get you out of my head. The world turns and days go by, but I'm not living them when you aren't by my side. We've spent so few moments together, but the ones we spend apart tear my heart to pieces. You *are* my happiness, Henry Quinn."

He grabbed me by my waist and hoisted me into the air, beaming as he spun me in a circle. I watched the starlight dance in his emerald eyes as we both released choruses of joyful laughter.

When my feet returned to the wooden planks of the docks, I placed a kiss on his cheek. He gave a gentle smile and his eyes traveled down to my lips, letting them linger there for one tantalizing moment. My breath hitched as he leaned towards me and my eyes fluttered shut, his soft kiss melting my heart. He kept one hand on my waist and the other found its way to my face, caressing my head just below my ear. I wrapped my arms around his neck. All that existed in that moment was Henry, our heartbeats, and the tranquil lull of the ocean waves surrounding us. I was lost in him; I could've stayed in that moment forever.

"Lillian!" The call came from the edge of the dock and I turned to see who had yelled for me, still blown away by the moment I had just experienced with Henry.

"Is that your brother?" Henry asked, looking down at me.

"I… think so," I said, walking towards the figure. "Ben?" I called.

"Lillian," he said, approaching, "Father knows you aren't home. I tried to stall him, but he went up to your room to wish you goodnight. He's out searching for you now. Mother's worried… You need to come home. I'm sorry."

I turned to Henry. "I'm sorry," I said.

"No," he told me, "go. We'll see each other again soon, I promise."

I nodded and Ben took my hand, rushing back towards the house. Adrenaline surged through my veins as I thought of a million scenarios. What would Father do this time? Would he find Henry and hurt him, too?

When we arrived back at home, though, Father was standing on the porch, waiting for my return. "Lillian," he said smoothly. "Have a good night out?"

17

Charlie

Aspen Hall, 1990

The next day, despite what I figured was my first-ever hangover, I decided to end things with Mike. It was an emotionally draining experience, but I knew that it had to be done, even if it meant Jonah would get the wrong idea. I woke up with an unbelievable headache and was certain I'd throw up if I moved more than an inch. I sat in my bed, completely still, for God knows how long.

The discolored, circular light in the center of the ceiling looked like it was spinning around me. I shut my eyes again, too nauseous to continue watching it.

Eventually, I summoned enough strength to stand up and put on a pair of sweatpants, the world swaying beneath my feet. I found a note taped to my dresser.

Meet me in the common room today at 2. We need to talk.

-Mike

"Ugh," I groaned, looking at my clock. I had twelve minutes before I was meant to go meet him. I sighed, knowing that what was to come would be an unpleasant conversation, at best.

Exiting my room, I made a beeline from my room to the elevator. The bright, fluorescent lights of the hallways burned my eyes and made my head pound even harder. *Just don't throw up*, I willed. *Don't throw up.*

When I got to the common room, Mike was already sitting on one of the couches, nervously toying with the seams of his Mariners jersey, lost in thought. "Hey, Mike," I said softly.

He jumped, clearly spooked. "Charlie," he said. "I didn't realize you were there. Sit."

"Look, Mike, I-" my ears started ringing. *Stay focused*. "I'm really sorry about last night, I was way out of line."

"It's fine." He said. "You were drunk, you weren't thinking clearly. I know you didn't mean what you said." He cleared his throat. "I wanted to meet you here so I could apologize, actually. I shouldn't have punched that guy. He wasn't worth it. I know you didn't actually want to kiss him; your judgment was clouded. You've told me that so many times."

"No, Mike."

He gave me a quizzical look.

"I remember everything I said. It was all true. I've not been entirely honest with you, and for that I'm so sorry," I said, trying to be as brave as I could with him.

"You mean you'd rather be dating that lanky band boy?"

"I hope you understand," I begged. "We can still be friends. I just... I don't think we should be any more than that."

"Goddammit!" Mike yelled. His booming voice was a hammer to my aching head. He stood and kicked the side of the brown leather couch. I lost my balance and slid to the edge. "I should've known. I should've dealt with this when I had a chance!" he continued frantically pacing.

"Mike, I-"

"No," he said, the intensity in his eyes burning through me. "Whatever you have to say, I don't want to hear it. I've had enough of you. I've had enough!" His voice raised to a shout and he slammed his fists against the nearest wall.

"Would you let me explain?" I said, my voice still quiet as I tried not to think about the pain seeping through my entire body.

Still breathing heavily, Mike nodded and sat down across from me, resting his elbows on his knees.

"Listen," I began. "I know that going out with you was wrong. I wasn't in the right place, you know, emotionally-"

"You liked the band boy."

I took a deep breath to keep myself from slapping him. "That's not the point. Let me finish."

"Sorry."

"I know what I did was wrong. I know I treated you badly. But I want you to know that I'm so, so eternally sorry for that..." I paused. "But I don't regret anything I said last night. We don't belong together, Mike. We aren't an amazing couple; we never would be. In your head, we've been dating for months. I've known you for a few weeks. It was never gonna work out."

Mike just sat there for a few seconds, dumbfounded. "I didn't realize," he said. "Sorry to get in the way of your perfect love story."

His mocking tone made my blood boil, but I was too tired and hungover to care. I shrugged. "I'm sorry too," I said, and walked off back to my room.

A few hours later, a knock came at my door and I sat up with a start. *Shit*, I thought to myself. *I was supposed to meet Jonah and Shane to work on that project!* "Just a second," I called, jumping out of bed and throwing on a sweatshirt. I tied my hair into some semblance of a ponytail and opened the door.

"Hey, Charlie," Jonah said.

"Hi," I replied, trying not to seem too flustered. "Come in. Ruby won't be back for a few hours. Where's Shane?"

He mindlessly dropped his backpack to the floor. "He's grabbing a few papers he accidentally left in his dorm, he'll be here in a couple of minutes." He hadn't pulled his eyes away from me since I opened the door. I gazed at them for a split-second, marveling at how they reflected the light through the window like pools of sweet honey.

"How's your nose?" I asked, remembering how Mike had tried to bash in his face just the night before.

"It's fine."

"I decided to break up with Mike," I told him, for no real reason and without a thought. We finally made eye contact, and my breath caught in my throat. It was as if I could see straight into his soul. For the past few weeks, I had longed for nothing more than a kiss from him, despite how I tried to convince myself otherwise. In spite of my efforts to stay away from him, I couldn't help but be somewhat glad that we were finally alone.

"Oh," he said. "I'm sorry." He didn't sound very apologetic, and he turned away from me.

"Don't be," I said, reaching for his hand, hoping he would face me. "It's better this-"

And then it finally happened. He whisked around faster than lightning, slamming my door behind him, wrapping his arm against my waist and pulling my body against his. He caught my eyes for just a moment before his lips finally collided with mine, and I felt something strong, something warm, something I had never felt before. His kiss was strong, hungry, and passionate, like the beginning of a symphony.

And then – *bam*.

The crescendo hit, our hearts pounding like dueling drums against one another, our bodies in one perfectly synchronized rhythm. He ran his fingers through my hair and my hands wandered all over his body. My knees began to shake, and he lifted me into his arms. I wrapped my legs around his body as his mouth shifted to my cheek, my ear, my neck, and all over. Eventually, he returned to my mouth, and my lips locked into his, finding the perfect groove.

Another knock came at the door and we pulled away from each other, trying to ignore the ever-growing magnetism surging in the air between us. I stared at him, my eyes sharp as knives. “Not a word of this,” I told him. “If my roommate finds out…”

“Shh,” he said, putting a finger to my lips. “Don’t worry. No one needs to know.”

“Okay.” I paused, then continued. “Come in, Shane,” I said, clearing my throat and fixing the mess my hair had become.

The door swung open and Shane stepped inside. “Okay,” he said, “who’s ready to talk about composition methods?”

18

Lillian

Adagio, Maine, 1934

"Father," I began, my voice quiet and shaky.

The wind began to pick up, clouds darkening the night. The lampposts cast my father's elongated shadow down the front staircase. "Lillian," he said a second time, his calm tone sending an eerie chill through my body.

Ben squeezed my hand and headed up the staircase. He tried to whisper something inaudible to my father but the man cut him off. "I trust you were just out on a harmless stroll," Father continued.

"Forgive me, Father," I said, starting up the staircase with a plea.

My father turned around and walked into the house, letting the door slam behind him. Ben and I exchanged worried looks and followed. My mind raced, trying to figure out what was going on in my father's head. "Father," I called to him, my voice ringing through the near-empty foyer.

He stopped in his tracks and turned to me. "What?" He asked sharply, and I sensed he was through discussing the matter.

"I – I didn't mean to upset you," I stammered, trying my best to remain steadfast.

He let out a long, exasperated sigh. "Of course, you upset me," he said, a slight vocalized laugh escaping his lips. "I want to know why you're so insistent on hiding things from me. I want to know what's gotten into that little head of yours, and I want to know why you feel compelled to fight me on every little thing!"

Tears formed in my eyes. I took a step towards him, praying that God would be on my side, just that one time. "I fight with you because you don't see me as your daughter. You don't see me as a woman with a heart and a soul, as someone who cares about her own life and happiness." I could no longer hold back my tears. "You see me as a puppet on a string, as someone you can manipulate until you get what *you* want!" I paused, my breath hitching.

I fell to my knees, my melancholy and fear suddenly overwhelming. I thought of Paul, and all the times my father had forced me to do something against my will. I thought of Henry, and the dreams I had for us. I thought of what Father would do to me if he ever found out. My voice softened, scarcely a whisper. "I'm sorry," I said, "Forgive me." Remembering that Ben was still standing in the corner, I hoped that maybe this time Father wouldn't hurt me, as he wouldn't want to upset his son.

The man said nothing. He walked towards me and stood above me, an unsettling grin appearing on his face. Kneeling down to my level, he glared at me, his ice-blue eyes meeting my own. His hand traveled through the air, the direct blow leaving a sharp sting against my cheek. "*Never* question me again," he growled in my ear as I lay there, helpless.

He stood up and spat on the ground, walking away from me. I sat up slowly, caressing my sore jaw. Within seconds, Ben was by my side.

"Are you alright?" he asked.

I nodded. "He scared me, is all." I paused. "Ben?"

"Yes?"

"You didn't... Father doesn't know where I was, does he?"

Ben shook his head. "When he noticed you were gone, I told him that you had gone out for a walk, that you couldn't sleep."

I threw my arms around him in a warm hug. "Thank you," I said, knowing that my punishment would've been much worse had Father known about my secret rendezvous.

"You're welcome," Ben told me. He scratched his head for a moment, pondering his next question. "So, Henry," he said. "You really care for him?"

I blushed. "I do."

"I'm glad," Ben replied. "You deserve to be happy… But know I'll be keeping an eye on him."

I nodded and smiled, grateful that I had someone like Ben looking out for me. "I'm going to go to bed," I told him as I hurried up the stairs and to my room. *Nothing will stop him*, I thought. *No matter how hard I fight, no matter what I do. It will always end like this.* That night, I knew there was no point in trying to hide from my Father, no point in bending to his will. No matter what I did, he would always find a reason to punish me. I couldn't wait to make it out of his grasp.

As far as he knew, I hadn't even done anything wrong that night. I had simply gone for a walk, and still, he found a way to get under my skin. He still didn't know that my relationship with Paul was over. And I didn't intend to inform him.

I was determined to continue to see Henry. And I would do exactly that.

I pulled some paper and an old fountain pen from my desk and sat by my window. I gazed out at the docks for a moment, watching a few boats pull into the harbor at the water's edge. I thought of Henry and the moment we shared together as I put pen to paper.

Dearest Henry,

I want to tell you how sorry I am that our time together tonight had to be cut short. I'd love to see you again soon, but I fear that my father will discover our relationship. If you wish to see me, I'll be taking a walk past the pub where we met on Wednesday at noon. If you happen to be walking by, I'm sure we could stop and talk for a while without being noticed. I miss you more and more every second we are apart. I wish only that we can someday spend every waking moment together, that you can hold me in your arms, and I can finally feel at home.

I'll see you in a few days, my dear.

Yours,

Lillian Abbott

I hid the letter away under my pillow and tried to fall asleep. *Someday*, I thought, *someday I'll be happy. Someday I'll escape this painful, mundane life. Someday, I will wake up each morning and be glad, for I will be blessed.*

19

Charlie

Pine Ridge University, 1990

"In conclusion," Shane said, "composers can take both a scientific approach or a more emotional, creative approach to composition of musical works. These methods are both effective in their own ways, but we've determined that taking a standpoint in which you utilize the best parts of each method would be the most effective."

We finished our presentation that morning with smiles on our faces. As the whole class applauded, Jonah and I exchanged excited looks, and Shane stood there, clueless, just taking it all in.

"Thank you," said our Music Theory professor, Dr. Brooks. "That was a riveting presentation, you three." He looked at his clipboard. "Cedar, Otto, and Declan," he said, "you're next."

We sat through the rest of the presentations with smiles on our faces, glad that the professor thought highly of our own. After class, I tagged along with Shane and Jonah to get some food before my violin lesson. We walked to the dining hall and sat down at a square table. I sat on one side, Jonah and Shane on the other.

Jonah and I still hadn't told anyone about our kiss. We wanted to keep our relationship quiet for as long as possible. I had no clue what would happen if Ruby were to find out that I was secretly going out with the guy she had a crush on. Shane, however, was proving that keeping our budding relationship under wraps was more difficult than we had imagined.

"Psst," he said that day at breakfast, elbowing Jonah.

"What?" Jonah whispered.

"Ten o'clock. Total babe."

I took a peek, and Shane was right. The girl walking past was *beautiful*. She had platinum blonde hair, caramel-colored eyes, and a figure that made me feel incredibly insecure. She had a way about her as she moved, an air of confidence that seemed to remind everyone just how incredible she was, in case they had somehow forgotten.

Even the pile of waffles she carried on her plate looked perfect.

Jonah just shrugged. “Go get her, then,” he said.

“Not really my type,” Shane said.

Jonah took a bite of his bagel. “That’s a shame.”

Shane looked at him, bewildered. “What are you doing?” he asked. “You were literally moping just a few days ago about how you’re single!”

Jonah avoided eye contact with him. I took a sip of water in the hopes neither of them would see me blushing. “I don’t know.” Jonah shrugged his shoulders. “Guess I’m over it.”

Shane dropped his spoon, a harsh *clang* ringing through the dining hall, and turned his head to face him. “You’ve found someone, haven’t you?”

“What? No!”

Shane stood up and stared me in the eyes. He smacked the table with one hand and pointed at me with the other. “You!” He said, all too enthusiastically.

“No!” We chorused.

He sat back down, looking disappointed, then narrowed his eyes and looked from Jonah, to me, then back to Jonah. “Okay,” he said. “But she’s been awfully friendly to us lately, and don’t think I don’t remember what you said the other night at that frat party.”

“Said what now?” I said.

“Don’t you remember?” Shane asked.

I shook my head.

“You were all *over* him. Told Mike you wanted to break up.”

“Oh,” I lied, “I don’t remember, I was drunk. But… Mike and I *did* break up.”

“Why?” Jonah asked, keeping up our façade.

“It just didn’t feel right,” I said. “I have to be more focused on school anyway. You know, to keep my scholarship.”

Shane gave me a look. “You broke up with him for school?” He stifled a chuckle. “Poor guy.”

“I didn’t break up with him *for school*,” I said, suddenly feeling defensive despite the underlying truth in Shane’s question. “It just wasn’t right. When someone is right, I’ll know.” I gave Jonah a look and he smiled at his half-eaten bagel.

“What was that look?” Shane said.

Jonah furrowed his brow. "What look?" He glanced my way once more and I blushed.

"*That* look!"

Jonah laughed him off. "Shane," he said, putting a hand on his friend's shoulder. "I think you're nuts."

A few days later, Jonah and I had dinner outside while we still could. Winter was fast approaching. I could feel a chill in the air; as November progressed, the Maine weather grew harsher and colder. We sat on a bench outside of Somerset Hall overlooking the open field where I first laid eyes on Jonah.

"So, Shane…" I began.

"What are we gonna do with him?" Jonah said with a laugh.

"He's gonna find out sooner or later."

"I'd rather push it off," Jonah said. "I've known Shane forever, he'll never let it go when he finds out."

I gave him a quizzical look. "I thought you met him in college."

He smiled. "No, we grew up together. Our parents were close when we were young, and I lost my mom at eleven…" he trailed off, then recollected himself. "So, yeah. We made a pact to come to college together."

I inched closer to him on the picnic bench. "Oh, Jonah, I'm sorry. I didn't know, I didn't mean to-"

"It's fine," he said, clearing his throat and scooping some pasta onto his plastic fork. "It was a long time ago. I'm over it."

"Still," I continued. "I'm sorry you had to go through that."

"It was alcohol poisoning," he said bluntly. I didn't know what to say, and Jonah continued. There was something resigned in his tone, as if he'd told the story so many times that he had somehow grown numb to the harrowing truth of it all. "My dad was working late one day, and I had stayed after school at a friend's house just a few blocks down. When I went home that day, she was already gone." He ran a hand through his wavy hair and straightened his bandana, as if that was his way of collecting himself. "So, yeah," He shrugged. "I don't drink. I'd rather make sure no one else gets into trouble like my mom did."

"Oh, Jonah," I said, placing a comforting hand on his leg. "That's terrible. I'm always here for you, you know that."

"Thank you." He kissed my forehead. "You don't need to worry about me, though, okay? Let me look out for you."

I smiled and took his hand. "As long as you're watching out for me, I'm watching out for you, too," I reminded him.

"If you insist," he said with a small chuckle.

We sat there and talked until I lost track of time. We lightened the mood. We talked about the silly things. Our favorite foods, our most embarrassing memories, guilty pleasures... We watched the sun set and the lampposts flicker on. I rested my head on Jonah's shoulder and he wrapped his arm around me, keeping me warm as the wind bit my skin. I took a deep breath and felt my eyelids begin to grow heavy, knowing I would soon have to go back to my room, but wishing I never had to leave his arms.

"You know, I never wanted to push you away," I told him, still feeling slightly guilty.

"I know."

"It's just, I'm only here because of my scholarship, and I've always been focused on school, only school, and now that I'm feeling the way I am, I don't know what to do..."

He shifted in his seat, leaned forward to look at me, and gave a teasing smile. "How is it, then," he asked, "that you're feeling?"

I blushed and gave him a playful push. "Oh, you know," I said.

He looked at me and tilted his head, like a puppy waiting for a treat, and I giggled.

"Like I really like you," I told him, my voice sobering. "In a way I've never liked anyone before."

His expression softened and he took my hand. "I feel the same way," he told me. "And I get it. You've got everything riding on your scholarship. I won't get in the way of that." He paused. "Promise."

"Okay." I smiled, leaning into him.

After a few more moments of watching nighttime creep onto campus, we finally decided to part ways. We stood outside the door to my room, wishing we weren't about to say goodbye, even if it was just for the night. He brushed a stray piece of hair from my face. I stood on my tiptoes and kissed him.

"Today was nice," I told him.

"It was," he agreed. "Good night, Charlie," he said, kissing me one more time.

"Good night." I unlocked my door and went inside, leaning against it once it clicked shut. I took a deep breath, reveling in the warm, fuzzy feeling I had inside.

"Damn," Ruby said.

I jumped, as I hadn't even realized she was in the room. "What?"

"Who's the lucky guy?"

"What are you talking about?"

She hopped off her bed and walked towards me, her perfectly curved figure gliding gracefully across the tiny dorm room. "Somebody kissed you today. It's written all over your face. Who is it?"

"Oh," I said, and laughed nervously. I thought back to a few days prior, when she had come into the room crying. Upon my asking what was wrong, she told me that Jonah had told her that their kiss was a mistake and he didn't want to be a couple. She cried on my shoulder for at least an hour that day. I couldn't break her heart again by telling her that *he* was my mystery man. "No one you know, don't worry," I lied. "He's just one of my music major friends."

"That's great!" She said excitedly. "I'm so happy for you!"

20

Lillian

Adagio, Maine, 1934

I sat near my window, watching, waiting, wishing I would soon see Henry walking around the back of the house. I heard footsteps echoing down the hall outside my room and my heart skipped a beat. *No one should be up at this hour,* I thought to myself, looking at the old clock on my wall. *It's ten minutes till midnight!*

I peeked my head out the door and looked down the hall. "Robert!" I said, my voice a fierce whisper.

He stopped in his tracks and turned to me. "What?"

"What are you doing up?"

"Well, I… I just…"

I gestured to him. "Come here," I said, "Don't wake Mother and Father."

It was only when he got to my room that I realized his face was red and blotchy, as if he had been crying. "Robert," I said, "What's wrong?"

He walked into my room and sat on the edge of my bed, taking a few deep breaths. "It's Father," he told me.

I wasn't surprised. I sat down beside him and rubbed his back, trying to calm him down. "You can tell me," I said. Robert had no clue about my… *complex* relationship with our father, and I didn't plan on telling him, not yet. I could, however, help him with whatever it was he was going through.

"It's Matthew," Robert said between hitched breaths. "Father's foreclosed on his family's home. He's selling it to someone else."

I tried my best to act as a voice of reason. This was usually Ben's job. "I'm so sorry, Robert," I said, pulling him in for a hug. "I know it's hard."

"It's not fair at all," he replied. "They're good people! And now, my first day working with Father, we took a house from my best friend and his family. They have no money, nowhere to go, and we stole the last thing they had."

"I understand," I said. "Father and I have had many disagreements as well. Maybe there's something we can do to help. For now, why don't you get some sleep? It's getting late."

He nodded, drying his eyes. "Thank you, Lily." He gave me another hug but pulled away quickly. "What was that?" he asked.

"What?"

"I heard something," he said, and walked over to my window.

"Robert, it was nothing, I'm sure," I urged, my heart pounding. What would Robert do if he knew about Henry?

"No, really! I think someone's down there. Could someone be stealing from Mother's vegetable garden?" He went over to the window and pushed it open. "Hello?" he called.

"Robert, get away from there!" I hissed, grabbing his arm and pulling him away.

"Lily, who's down there?"

"Lower your voice," I told him. "It's Henry."

"The boy you met in a pub?"

"Shh!"

"Sorry."

"Yes," I said. "Ben told you about him?"

Robert nodded. "He told me not to say anything, though. He said you've been going out to see him and that's why I wasn't supposed to say anything if I saw you." My brother took a momentary pause. "And he said that we had to make sure Mother and Father don't find out. Ben really does seem to like him, though."

"So, you *promise* you won't say a word to our parents?" I looked at him intensely.

"Cross my heart."

"Thank you," I said. "Now get yourself to bed and stay quiet!"

He nodded and hurried off. I wrapped myself in a shawl and rushed downstairs, hoping I hadn't kept Henry waiting for too long. During the course of the past two months, we had been seeing each other in secret, mostly away from the house and through our secret letters. That night was different, though. I wanted to invite him inside. I was getting too tired of only seeing him during our occasional walks near Sixth Avenue, only where we were sure none of my father's little cronies would see us. It was time for us to take the next step, even if it meant entering the belly of the whale.

I left the house through the side door and rounded the corner towards Mother's garden. "Henry!" I said quietly, catching sight of him sitting on a large rock on the outskirts of the garden.

"Lillian!" Excitement lined his voice and he leapt to his feet. He rushed towards me and swept me into an affectionate embrace.

I hugged him back and whispered to him, "Come inside. We just have to be careful, so my father doesn't see us."

"You're sure it's okay?"

"Yes. They're all asleep." I took his hands. "I want you to come inside now, Henry."

He nodded and we went inside. I led him through the back hallway, through the parlor and had nearly made it to the staircase by the time I realized he was no longer behind me. "Henry?" I called out quietly, making sure not to let my voice resonate too loudly through the echo-prone halls.

I slipped back through the parlor doors and saw him standing at our grand piano which sat towards the back corner of the parlor, near a half-open window adorned with sheer cream-colored curtains that waved about in the wind.

Pulling my shawl tighter against me, I leaned against the wall and watched him marvel at the instrument.

Ever so gently, he brushed his fingers against the keys, his face just inches away from the piano's surface. His hand traveled from the keys to the lid as he admired the handiwork of the piano's most ornate details.

"Do you like it?"

He jumped, as if he had been completely lost in his own world. His hand flew to his heart. "Yes," he breathed, sounding much calmer than he looked. "It's incredible."

"You can play it," I told him, stepping out of the doorway and into the parlor. "I don't think anyone will wake." I wasn't sure how true my statement was, but I hadn't heard Henry play since the day we met, and my heart yearned to hear his marvelous melodies once more. I knew there was no guarantee of safety, but I prayed we could share this moment, just this one, in peace.

He reached out his hand. "Come," he said. "Sit."

I joined him on the seat and watched him play for a while. I had never seen someone with such a pure love and passion for their craft. It was as if the music flowed from his heart into his veins, through his fingertips and out into the world. Chills ran through my body as I took it all in.

Henry was so full of heart, full of passion, full of love. More than anything, he *cared.* He cared about everything, so deeply, so unconditionally. Watching him in that moment, I felt as if I had found what I'd spent my whole life searching for. I found someone who cared.

"Do you sing?" he asked, the tempo of his music slowing.

"What?"

He stopped playing and looked at me, his expression softening. "I said, 'do you sing?'" he repeated.

I shook my head, suddenly blushing. "Oh, no," I said. "Not me. My older sister is the artist of the family."

He narrowed his eyes and put his arms around me. "You're a poet, though."

"I am," I responded.

"Then you're an artist just the same," he said, his hands returning to the piano, resting delicately on the keys. "You can do it. Pretend you're writing a poem, but as the words flow through you, they become more than just words. They become a melody," he explained.

"Well, what should I sing about?" I asked him, nervously toying with a loose strand of blonde hair.

"Sing about things you care about," he said, his music slowly starting to fill the room again. "Sing about the gentle crash of the ocean waves, or the chirping of a songbird breaking through the silence of the morning, or..."

"Or pianists with brilliant eyes and the sweetest smiles?"

He tried not to show it, but I could see him blushing. "If that's what strikes your fancy."

"It is," I said.

And so, that night, sitting in the parlor under the yellow light of my mother's favorite lamp, we wrote a song together. We put our heads and our hearts together and created a work of art, *our* work of art.

"That was phenomenal," Henry said when we'd had enough. Then, quieter, he continued. "*You're* phenomenal. You have the voice of an angel."

I beamed and leaned in for a kiss. Henry's lips met mine, and it was as if the fireworks from our very first kiss had reignited.

"Having fun, are we?"

In an instant, my heart dropped to the floor. *Father's awake.*

21

Charlie

A parking lot, Pine Ridge University, 1990

"How many Bon Jovi cassettes do you have?" I asked Jonah with a laugh, rooting through the music stash in his car.

"Hey, don't judge me," he said with a smile, popping in one of the many tapes.

We laughed together as he rounded a corner, the brakes of his dad's old Volkswagen Jetta resistant. I grabbed onto the side of the car door and hollered, "Oh my God!"

"Sorry," he said, "I need to get these brakes checked!"

"How far is the movie theater?" I asked him, watching the trees in all their various colors whisk by through the window at breakneck speed.

He looked at me, eyes widening. “Um…”

“Jonah…”

“Okay, so I don’t actually know where it is,” he said. “Do you?”

“I grew up in Adagio!” I said with a laugh. “I live in the middle of nowhere, I don’t know where anything is out here!”

“I live three hours away, too,” Jonah replied, “so neither do I!”

Within the next ten minutes, we ended up driving down some tiny dirt trail that I’m pretty sure was private property. The little Jetta bounced up and down with every bump in the narrow path. Jonah and I struggled to keep it together, laughing to the point of tears.

He eventually pulled over. “Where do you think we are?” I asked, getting out of the car.

“I have no clue.” He slammed his car door shut and looked out across the horizon. “It’s really nice out here, though.”

I agreed. Somehow, we had ended up next to a wide field framed with trees of various colors, all sorts of wildflowers sprinkled throughout the lush green grass. “Come on.” I took his hand. We walked through the field together, no longer caring that we wouldn't see a movie that day.

Jonah stopped in his tracks and plucked some blue wildflowers from the ground. He tucked them behind my ear in my hair. "Perfect," he said, placing a tender kiss on my cheek. "You look beautiful."

God, you're charming, I thought to myself. "Thank you," I said.

He grabbed me by the waist and spun me around. I felt like a princess in some sort of fairy tale, no longer having a care in the world other than him. When I was with Jonah, we were the only two people on the planet. I didn't have a Music Theory test to worry about, no homework to make up, no studying to do. I just had Jonah. And he was all I needed.

We were caught up in each other when the skies opened up and thunder crashed. The rain was just a tiny sprinkling at first, and Jonah continued to kiss me, not wanting to pull away. An inexplicable warmth filled me to the brim, blossoming inside my chest like dozens of wildflowers beginning to bloom. Then, suddenly, as if Mother Nature wanted to remind us that we had other things to attend to, the sprinkling became steady rain, which erupted into torrential downpour. As buckets of cold rain poured down on us and we broke out into helpless laughter yet again, Jonah grabbed my hand and the two of us ran back to his haphazard little Volkswagen, nearly slipping as the rain formed puddles on the ground beneath our feet.

"Here," Jonah said, popping the trunk. "Climb in."

He handed me a half-eaten bag of chips and an old sweatshirt, and we sat in that open trunk for at least an hour, just talking and watching the rain beat steadily against the windows.

At one point amidst our uncontrollable laughter, I took a deep breath and gazed into his golden eyes. Loose strands of hair stuck to his face with rainwater, and the shoulders of his gray t-shirt were darkened with water.

"What?" He asked, noticing that I had quieted.

"Nothing," I said, blushing.

"Not nothing," he replied, smoothing down my hair with his calloused hand.

I took his hand and kissed it. "This is just… perfect."

He chuckled. "I wouldn't exactly say that," he replied. "I mean, I got us lost, we missed the movie, and I nearly killed us with my piece-of-trash car, but…"

"Exactly," I replied. "It's romantic."

He looked bewildered. "Explain to me, Charlie Quinn, how getting lost and nearly crashing the car is romantic."

"Because we're out here, all alone, amidst what some would call disaster, and all I can think about is you."

When the rain finally cleared up enough to drive safely, we somehow navigated our way back to campus, random Bon Jovi tapes becoming the soundtrack to our trip, laughing through our pristine rendition of "I'll Be There for You." I thought I heard some muffled shouts when we pulled into Jonah's parking spot, but I couldn't quite make them out.

"He's got us," Jonah said with a sigh, putting his hand on my thigh.

"What?"

He pointed towards a familiar blonde figure twirling a red and white umbrella in his hands, despite the fact that the rain had ceased. "Damn kid figured it out."

"Kid?" I asked with a laugh, "Isn't he older than you?" Shane approached and started tapping on Jonah's window.

"Eh, only by, like, a month. He acts like one, anyway," Jonah replied, rolling the window down. "Hey, you," he said.

"I knew it!" Shane hollered. "I knew it, and you guys tried to hide it from me, but I knew it *all* along! Why didn't you tell me?"

Jonah shook his head and got out of the car. "What are you talking about, Dude?"

"What do you mean, what am I talking about? This is actual, real-life proof that you two are dating! I've been saying it for weeks now!"

"I just don't know what you're talking about, Shane," I said, joining Jonah on the sidewalk. The three of us started walking towards the suite houses where Shane and Jonah lived.

"What do you *mean*?" Shane was getting comically frustrated, and Jonah and I found it ridiculously funny.

"What do *you* mean?" Jonah countered.

"I *mean* that you two are most definitely a couple!"

"Now that is a preposterous accusation," Jonah told him as we continued walking. He looked at me and winked. Upon my quizzical look, he pulled me close and kissed me, right on the lips, with Shane just a few paces ahead of us, completely oblivious to our actions.

Shane stopped when he realized we had been quiet for a few seconds. "Guys," he said, turning around. "Guys!"

His eyes widened and he pointed at me, then at Jonah, and back to me, a strange sound of confusion and pride escaping his lips. "I *knew* it!"

"We just didn't want to risk what we had," Jonah said, turning back to Shane. "You get it, right?"

Shane nodded. "Yeah, of course I do." His voice went all squeaky and he pulled Jonah in for a tight hug. "I'm so proud of you, Bro," I heard him whisper. "You finally got a good one."

"Glad you approve," I said to him, putting my arm around Jonah's waist.

Shane nodded. "Don't you go breaking his heart, now," he said, wagging a finger at me. "And you-" he turned to Jonah – "don't you screw this up either." He paused. "When are we telling the rest of the guys?"

"Whoa, whoa," Jonah said. "Who said anything about telling the guys?"

"Well, you guys can't just keep something like this to yourselves!"

"Shane, that's kind of the whole point. It's what we've been doing this whole time," Jonah replied, smiling down at me, "and it's been working out great."

"Aww, you guys," Shane said. He paused, and his expression sobered. "Do you actually think I'm gonna be able to hide this?"

"Can you just try?" I asked. "For us?"

"Ugh, fine," Shane agreed. "But only because I love you guys. And because I *really* want this to work out!" He seemed as giddy as a schoolgirl.

"Thank you," Jonah said. "We appreciate it."

"You know I'm not gonna last long," he said as we started walking again. "It's just too exciting, I won't be able to contain myself, I..."

I laughed, finally realizing just why Jonah had been so hesitant to tell Shane that we had been dating. Jonah's fingers interlocked with my own as we walked down the path, Shane's ramblings becoming background noise. Something told me we didn't have to worry about people finding out about us. Something told me this was right.

22

Lillian

Adagio, Maine, 1934

“Who is this?"

Stand your ground. “This is Henry,” I said. “He was actually just leaving.”

“Henry,” my father hissed, gliding across the parlor towards us. I put a protective arm in front of Henry, resting my hand on his.

“Yes, Sir?”

“What are you doing in my parlor?”

“Well, Sir, I was just… Um…” Henry stammered and looked at me.

"I invited him in, Father," I interrupted.

He glared at me. "Quiet, Lillian," he said. "I'm talking to your little friend here."

"Mr. Abbott, I was just enjoying your daughter's company," Henry tried. "You've raised a truly amazing young woman."

While I appreciated his compliment, I didn't look at him. My body remained stiff, tense with fear. My father gave a sardonic chuckle and pulled Henry to his feet by grabbing a fistful of his shirt. "Don't patronize me," he spat in his face.

Henry nodded. I remembered how brave he was when he stood up for me at the pub, hoping that same valor would help him hold his ground against my father. "My apologies," he said. "I'll just be going now." He started towards the door.

"Henry!"

He turned back around at the sound of my father's voice.

"I don't want you near my daughter *ever* again, do you understand?"

He nodded.

"Now get out of my house, you impoverished, destitute, piece of Sixth Avenue scum!"

"Father!"

Upon hearing my shout, my father's rage became too much to hide. Despite Henry still standing in the doorway, he grabbed me by the shoulders and tossed me to the ground. A well-placed kick to my stomach sent me reeling. My vision blurred and I gasped for air.

When I opened my eyes, expecting to see Father staring down at me, I instead witnessed Henry grab him by the shoulder and pull him away from me. "Henry, no!" I cried.

"Young man," my father said, collecting himself, unfazed by Henry's heroic move. "I thought it was clear that you don't belong in my daughter's life."

"Sir, all due respect, but I think it's more likely that violence from her father is the thing that doesn't belong."

I caught my breath and managed to stand.

"Watch your tongue," Father snapped. "and get the bloody hell out of my house!"

Henry didn't argue anymore, he just shot me a longing look and left the house. I called to him and stepped forward, but Father put himself between us, blocking my way.

His eyes remained glued to the door even after Henry shut it. I didn't dare move. "Get to bed," he said. "I'll deal with you tomorrow."

"Father-"

"Go," he said, "before I change my mind."

When I finally made it to my room that night, I struggled to process everything that had happened. All I could think about was Henry. Father now knew all of my secrets. He knew and he would never let Henry step foot near me again.

I could no longer hold back my tears. Big, ugly sobs took over my body. I was given happiness for just a fleeting moment, only to have Father tear it away again the second he was given the opportunity.

I heard a knock come against the wall closest to my bed. It was a sequence of knocks I hadn't heard in a long time, a secret code of sorts that Ben and I had created when we were just kids. When one of us needed the other, we would knock on the wall connecting our two rooms. I took a deep breath and tried to dry my eyes before I walked into his room.

"Sorry if I woke you," I said to him.

Ben shook his head. “I was already awake,” he replied, standing up from the chair in the corner of his room. “Come here.” He held out his arms and I ran into them.

“He told Henry to never come back,” I said with a sob.

“Shh, shh…” My brother rubbed circles along my back. “Calm down, Lily.” He held onto my shoulders and looked into my eyes. “Sit with me.”

We sat together on his bed, just like I had done with Robert a few short hours earlier. “I snuck Henry into the house,” I said. “I know I shouldn’t have, but I couldn’t think of a better way to see him.”

There was overwhelming sympathy in Ben’s eyes. “It’s okay that you made a mistake,” he explained. “It isn’t over. You and Henry certainly aren’t over. This is just a little bump in a very long road.” He paused, noticing that I was beginning to calm down. “This isn’t the end, Lily,” he said. “You’ll come back from this.”

I nodded, wiping the tears from my eyes. “Thank you for everything, Benny.”

“Of course.” He gave me another hug, helping me feel even the slightest bit of hope again.

I walked back to my room and checked my clock before collapsing into bed. It was about 4:15 a.m. I wasn't thrilled to have to wake up in just three short hours, but once I finally made it to my bed for the night, sleep consumed me immediately. I awoke the next morning feeling fine, aside from knowing that my father was bound to punish me for what I had done with Henry.

23

Charlie

Pine Ridge University, 1990

My mind raced as I tried to answer the final few questions on my first-ever college exam. My hands were coated in sweat and my knees shook as I slowly came to the realization that I had no clue what I was doing. I looked around the lecture hall, suddenly noticing that everyone else was frantically writing down answers. *Oh, God,* I thought to myself, *what am I doing?*

My face flushed with warmth and my vision began to blur as tears filled my eyes. The blank page of my exam was glaring at me, taunting me, reminding me that I had made the conscious decision to spend time with Jonah the day before instead of spending time with my textbooks.

“That’s it,” said Dr. Brooks. “Bring your exams up front, please, face down on the podium.”

I said nothing, walking up to the podium as if in some sort of trance. I didn’t stop to see Jonah and Shane after class. I just walked back to Aspen as quickly as my legs would carry me.

I fumbled with my key, hands still shaking, as I opened my door and went into my room, beyond grateful that Ruby wasn’t there. I collapsed into my bed and grabbed my pillow, squeezing it tight and taking deep breaths. I don’t know how long it took for me to calm down, but it was a long time. I ended up pacing in circles around the small perimeter of the room, trying to think of what would happen if I failed my Music Theory class.

I started to shake again, my fear of failure overtaking me once more. I sat on the ground on the center of the floor, bringing my knees to my chest and trying to breathe. I tried to push the invasive thoughts out of my head, tried to convince myself that it didn’t matter.

But what if I wasn’t good enough to be a music major?

“Fresh air,” I muttered to myself, grabbing my key and heading out of my room. I walked mindlessly around campus for at least an hour, maybe more, trying to figure out what to do with myself.

"Mom?" I said into the payphone.

"Sweetheart!" my mom shouted, sounding so excited to hear from me.

Tears welled up in my eyes again upon hearing her voice. I hadn't realized how much I had missed her in the four short weeks I had been at school. "Hi, Mom," my voice cracked.

"What's wrong, Charlie?" she asked, her voice suddenly soft and sympathetic.

"I just failed a music test," I said plainly, trying to take deep breaths so my mom could understand what I was saying.

She was silent for a moment, so I continued. "I don't know what happened, I just feel like maybe I didn't study enough, but what if this means I don't belong in the music program? What if I'm just not good enough and I shouldn't be here?"

"Shh, shh," she said. "Calm yourself down. How much time did you spend studying?"

"I don't know." I was still weeping.

"Then maybe you should study more next time, that's all," my mom scolded, and paused. "Remember why you're there, Charlie."

"I know, Mom."

"Don't get distracted. Stay focused."

"I will."

"Charlie?"

"Yeah?"

"Don't let it happen again."

I hung up the phone and headed to the music building, still trying desperately to calm myself down. I walked into the storage locker and pulled out my violin, hoping that practicing my music would help me to win some confidence back.

Thoughts of Jonah entered my mind. I remembered how we had spent the weekend gallivanting around in his Jetta, ignoring everything but each other. Guilt racked my body. I had ruined everything. My feelings had gotten in the way, just as mother had warned me.

Our music building had three different concert halls. My favorite had a round stage and only two hundred red padded seats in the audience, and the acoustics were perfect for a solo violin. I pulled it out of its case and ran my fingers across the light spruce wood.

It was my namesake's violin. She had gifted it to me when I was very young. I lifted the instrument to my neck and readied the bow. I took a deep breath and began to play. *This one's for you, Great-Aunt Charlotte.*

Memories of her filled my head as I filled the empty concert hall with my music. I remembered the day I first mentioned playing the violin. It was Christmas Day, 1976, when I was only four years old. We had all gathered at her house for a homemade meal, and she had burnt the food because she had run upstairs to get the violin instead of watching the ham. I remembered Great-Uncle Timothy laughing with Grandpa Henry about something I didn't quite understand. I remembered Great-Aunt Charlotte handing me the instrument, warning me to be careful with the delicate bow. I remembered the chorus of joyful laughter as I played my first note that day, my grandparents cheering the loudest of all.

I wanted nothing more than to make her proud with my music, and that day, as I stood alone on the stage, I played for her, and for her memory.

I played to remind myself that music ran within my veins, that it was a part of me and a part of my family.

But something still felt wrong. If I was really made for music, why did I fail such an important exam? Was I really so careless as to let a boy distract me from school?

Was this really what I was meant to do?

24

Lillian

Adagio, Maine, 1934

A knock came at my door when I was meant to be waking up that day. I yawned and stretched, watching the early morning light slanting through the window. “Lillian,” he called in. “your mother needs you in the kitchen.”

“Yes, Father,” I replied. I had managed to stay on his good side for the greater part of three weeks. “Tell her I’ll be down in a few moments.” I tucked my pen away in the drawer of my desk and gathered up the last two pages of my letter. I was just hiding them away when the door to my room swung open.

“Now, Lillian,” he said.

"Okay." I fumbled and one of the pages slipped from my hands.

"What's this?" He picked it up from the ground.

"Oh, it's nothing," I said, trying to take the page from him.

He snatched it from my grasp. "I don't think this is nothing," he determined. "It says, 'Alone in my bed, I sit here and think of you. I long for my hand to be in yours, for our hearts intertwined-'"

I blushed. "Father, please."

He continued to read. "'I dream of you and I wish for you, my one and only love.' Don't tell me these letters are for that Sixth Avenue pauper?"

I took the page from him. "His *name* is Henry," I said, "and people are worth more than just the pennies in their pockets."

He scoffed and, without warning, opened my desk drawer where I had stashed all of the letters Henry had written for me. He laughed and lifted the stack of paper from the drawer. "'My darling Lillian, forgive me, for I fight to find the right words to tell you what it is I wish to say. I hope to someday be with you without any risk of being found, for you to be safe, safe in my arms forever. None other has touched my heart as you have. You are my sun and my moon, you are my muse.' How...*sweet*." The word was vile coming from my father's mouth. He continued to shuffle through the array of pages. "What's this?"

"What's what?"

"'On Friday, the 16th of November, I ask that you meet me by the docks where we shared our first kiss. I need to be with you, and I'm ready to leave everything behind so we can start anew. Together.'" He paused as it dawned on him. "You were going to run away together? Tonight?" His voice had become extremely calm, so much so that it was eerie, unsettling.

I nodded, knowing full well that there was no way out of this.

He threw the letters back in my face, disgust and contempt in his eyes. "I thought you'd have learned the words 'never again' after last time," he scolded.

I tried collecting them from the floor, pages and pages of discourse between Henry and I from the past few weeks. After he'd found us in the parlor that night, I had done my best to keep our continued relationship hidden from Father. I had succeeded until that morning.

He turned and started to leave, stopping in the doorway. "Come to think of it, I'm sure your mother can make do without you in the kitchen today. It will be best, I think, if you stayed in your room for a while." He took the hidden key from atop my dresser.

"Father, please-"

He shushed me and continued. "I'd rather not listen to you anymore right now," he said, walking towards the door. "I gave you a romantic opportunity with a perfectly nice young man."

"You did not give me an opportunity!" I said, my anger escalating. "You knew Paul was wrong for me, you knew it would never work. That's why you didn't care that he didn't have money."

My father chuckled. "Quite the opposite," he said, unfazed by the display of emotion in my voice. "Paul was about to inherit his family's fortune after the untimely death of his father. He would've been a perfect match for you, if you hadn't squandered it with your ramblings about true love and soulmates." Father paused to clear his throat. "Now, I think it would be best for you to spend the day in here, alone, thinking about how you've betrayed my trust with plans to run away from the great future I've planned for you." He didn't give me the chance to respond before he whisked away, out of the room, locking the door behind him.

I pounded on the door, trying to open the knob, wishing it didn't only lock from the outside. Tears filled my eyes and I began to sob. "Father, please! I won't run, just let me out! Please!"

"Father, why-" I could hear Robert's voice outside of my door.

"It's nothing, Son," he replied. "Your sister just has some thinking to do."

"Father!" I called, knowing he was still loitering just outside. "Father, don't you understand how I ache? Can't you imagine how hurt I feel?"

"Can you imagine how betrayed I feel?" he said coldly. "My own daughter, betraying my trust, planning to run from me? Why would you do such a thing?"

I didn't answer straight away and rested all of my weight against the door, taking a deep breath. "Because I *love* him, Father!" I cried, voice cracking. "Do you know what that feels like? Or are you incapable of such a thing?"

He pushed open the door with such force, it sent me careening across the room, my body slamming against the wall. Before I had time to think, he dragged me to my feet and berated me with punches, striking me once, twice, what felt like a thousand times. I tucked myself into the corner of my room and curled into a ball, shaking, crying.

"Never," Father seethed, "*never* question me like that again."

I nodded sheepishly, not moving from my little corner.

A few hours later, when I was certain Father had gone, I rose to my feet and walked to my desk, ready to write one last letter, ready to escape the misery of this house once and for all.

Dear Benny,

I'm leaving tonight. I won't be coming back. I'm going to live with Charlotte for a while, and I'm taking Henry with me. If you need me, write to her.

I want to thank you for everything. Thank you for protecting me for so long, for watching out for me, for keeping my secrets. Watch out for Robert, Sammy, and Mary for me. Keep them safe, as I'm sure you will. Tell them I love them, and I miss them.

Make sure you write to me. I love you.

With love,

Lily

I folded it into thirds and placed it on my pillow with a kiss, hoping Ben would find it before Father. I sat by my window and waited for the sun to set, for Henry to appear.

"Psst! Lillian!" I awoke at the sound of his voice outside my window. I don't even remember dozing off.

"Henry!" I pushed my curtains out of the way and leaned out the second-story window, looking down at him.

"What are you waiting for?" he asked. "Come down."

"I'm locked in my room!" I said. He disappeared from my view. "Henry? What are you doing?"

Henry reappeared in front of me, climbing up the trellis that framed my half open window. He leaned in through my window and placed a quick kiss on my lips. "Come on," he said, and wrapped his arm around my waist, steadying me for the climb. "Step carefully."

We arrived back on firm ground and I noticed Henry's younger brother standing a few feet away. "Hi, Miss," he said. "I'm sorry for stealing from your garden, and…" he scratched his head nervously. "I'm sorry I have to tag along with you and Henry. I… I just don't have a place…"

I put a hand on his shoulder, marveling at how much he looked like his brother. "It's okay," I said. "You're Henry's family. You're important to me now, too."

"Thank you."

Henry picked up his lantern and looked at me, his smile turning sour when he saw the bruises I wore. "Lillian," he said softly, his gentle hand grazing my face, "what happened?"

"My father happened." I looked away.

"Oh. I'm sorry."

"No," I said, taking his hand. "I'm sorry." I paused. "Come on, let's get out of here. My sister lives just south of here, all we have to do is follow the coastline."

He nodded and we began our journey, hand in hand, guided by the light of his lantern.

25

Charlie

Pine Ridge University, 1990

I sat on the edge of the stage when I'd had enough of playing, holding my head in my hands and my violin bow in my lap.

"Charlie!" His voice startled me and I looked up. Jonah. "There you are," he said, his voice oozing with relief. "I've been looking for you for hours, I was so worried! Where have you been?" He arrived at the edge of the stage and scooped me up in a great big hug. "What's wrong?" he asked.

I shook my head. "Nothing. It's just been a really long day." My voice cracked and I started to cry, too frustrated with myself to even be embarrassed about my reddening face.

"Hey," he said, pulling me tight against him and kissing the top of my head. "Deep breaths. Talk to me."

"I'm just not sure I should even be in the music program anymore," I told him. "That test was terrible, and if I can't even handle that, what kind of music teacher will I be?"

He shook his head and smiled. "Nonsense," he said. "the test was unbelievable; I'd be surprised if anyone gets above a C. And you, Charlotte Quinn, are one of the greatest musicians I've met in my life." He paused, then added, "And I've met Jon Bon Jovi."

I gave a pained laugh and wiped away my tears. "Thanks." I looked up at him, my expression still troubled and distant.

"Come sit with me," he said, sitting in one of the velvet seats of the concert hall, inviting me to join him. "Tell me what's wrong."

"Jonah, I just don't think I'm doing the right thing."

"So, you bombed one test."

I sniffled and nodded.

He looked deep into my eyes and smiled knowingly. "That doesn't define who you are as a musician, Charlie." He toyed with his favorite strand of my hair right by my temple. "You could have a million years' worth of knowledge in here..." He said, sliding his finger down to my chest, "but what matters is what's in here." He rested his finger on my chest for a split-second and my heart skipped a beat. "Your passion. And if there's one person in the world with passion... It's you."

I turned my head from him. "Jonah, I..."

"You belong in this program. One bad test doesn't mean it's the end."

"What if it means it's the end of... of this?" I ran my fingers through my hair, toying with a strand near my shoulder, refusing to look at Jonah.

His eyes widened; he looked at me, bewildered. "What do you mean?" He reached a finger towards my face to lift up my chin, but I turned in my seat. Jonah sunk away for a moment, dejected.

"I mean, maybe... What-what if this was a mistake?" I gestured to the space between us, where a little brown armrest sat between us. "What if I'm too distracted, what if this wasn't the right choice for me?" I bit back a sob.

"Charlie, what are you saying?" He reached for my hands, but I pulled away from him again, tears filling my eyes.

"I promised my mom that I would do everything in my power to focus on school. And I…" My breath caught in my throat as I tried to figure out what I was trying to say. "I haven't been doing that. I've been too focused on you. I told you I was nervous about this, that's why I insisted I couldn't be with you before, and I thought that had changed, I really did, but… I don't think it has. I'm still having doubts. I... I think I need to take a break."

His face twisted with emotion. Looking at him through eyes clouded by tears, I couldn't tell if he was angry, sad, or both. I stood up to leave, too afraid of what he was going to say. My mother's voice echoed in my head. *Don't get distracted. Stay focused.* I headed back towards the stage, grabbed my violin, and headed for the door.

"Charlie, wait," he said. "Please."

I stopped in my tracks, hating the fact that I had upset him. I cared so deeply for him, I didn't want to hurt him, but what else could I do? "I need some space, Jonah," I said, my voice breaking.

"No." His voice was firm, stern. "You need me."

I whirled around and glared at him, my blue eyes sharp as daggers. "What did you just say?" I asked, my sadness escalating into blind rage.

"I didn't mean it like that, you know I didn't. I just mean-"

"You think I can't do this on my own?" I advanced towards him, suddenly enraged by his assumption.

"No, you definitely can," he said, taking a step back. "I just mean that I want us to be a team." He bumped into the row of seats and steadied himself, trying to look nonchalant, but his voice started to shake as he spoke. "And if that means that school has to come first, fine. If it means we go out less so you can study, fine. If it means I have to wait for you for days, or for weeks, or for months, *fine*. I'll wait as long as it takes. I... I just want to be here for you. I tried so hard to get here, Charlie. I can't give up now. I can't give up on *us*."

He's fighting for me, I thought, and that warm feeling returned to my stomach. I cleared my throat, knowing I couldn't just show him how joyful I truly felt. "I don't know, Jonah."

"But I *do* know." He moved closer to me.

"You know what?" I crossed my arms.

"That I love you."

His words lingered in the air between us as I stood there, taken aback. I didn't what to say, what to do, what to think, and, for a moment, I let my heart soar with the thought that we could really make it through these issues together. My eyes widened and I just stood still, dumbfounded, staring at him, trying not to combust as a thousand emotions bubbled up inside of me. "I-I don't know what to say," I finally said, putting in a conscious effort not to scream the words back at him.

He said it again. "Charlie, I love you, and I'll do everything I can to convince you of that. Just give me a chance." He paused for a moment and collected himself. "Do you love me?"

The angry fire raging inside of my chest washed away with his words. Maybe Jonah wasn't the problem, but the solution. "Yes," I said, moving towards him slowly. I nodded and took in a breath. "You're right." I tried to suppress the grin that teased its way onto my face as I looked at him, knowing that everything he had said had been the truth. "I love you."

Suddenly, he grabbed my face with both hands and kissed me, and all of that fire, anger, rage and passion I had felt in the past few moments exploded inside of me. I tore off his bandana and sunk my fingers into his thick, chestnut colored hair as he swept his tongue between my lips, our bodies intertwining.

And then the door swung open, light spilling into the empty concert hall.

And yet again, we were pulled apart.

"Oh, great, you finally found her!" Shane's voice echoed from the back of the concert hall as he walked between rows of seats and sat down in the first row. "Okay, so…" he began.

Jonah rolled his eyes and gave his best friend a knowing look. Despite his obvious frustration, there was an ease about the exchange that told me he had given his best friend that same look a hundred – no, a *thousand* – times. "Shane, what did you-"

"The rest of the guys found out about you two." He continued quickly, defending himself, before Jonah could snap at him. "They kept asking where you were, and they were gonna go knock on your door, and I just *may* have let it slip that you were out looking for Charlie..."

Jonah looked at me, then back to his friends. "That's okay," he said, to my surprise. "They can know." He paused, as if considering what he had just said, then turned to me. "Right?"

I gazed at that goofy smile, all of my doubts about our relationship evaporating. "Yeah," I said. "We'll worry about Ruby later." I gave him a quick peck on the cheek.

"Okay, you little lovebirds," Shane said loudly. "I'll be waiting in the lobby when you're done canoodling."

Jonah and I broke into fits of laughter, our foreheads still pressed against one another. "We're coming, Shane," I said. I stood up and packed away my violin, and Jonah grabbed his bandana from the floor. We followed Shane out of the concert hall.

Declan, Otto, and Cedar were standing in the lobby, apparently anxiously awaiting Jonah's arrival. I blushed as we entered and they engaged in choruses of "Get it!" and "Look at you, Bro!"

Cedar was the first to stop the rabble. "Shh, gentlemen," he said, his voice echoing in the vast room. "We have a lady in our midst."

I laughed as Cedar stepped forward and kissed my hand, like a prince would've done back in medieval times. "Milady," he said in a terrible fake British accent, "I hereby offer you a formal invitation to spend Thanksgiving at the honorable residence of the Jameson household." Upon noticing my confused expression, he dropped character and continued. "We all spend Thanksgiving at my place, it's a tradition. You can come if you want."

"Oh," I said, glancing at Jonah, who nodded earnestly. "Okay? I'll be there, I guess."

The four guys jumped up and down excitedly, and I tried to hold back my laughter at the sight of their shenanigans. Jonah put his arm around my waist. “Looks like you’re one of us now,” he said.

“Looks like,” I agreed.

26

Lillian

Outskirts of Adagio, Maine, 1934

I knocked three times on the front door of Charlotte's little seaside cottage just past Adagio. No answer. I knocked again.

A man opened the door, still wearing a robe and slippers. "Hello?"

"Norman!"

"Lillian? Is that you?"

I nodded. "Yes, it's me," I said to my sister's husband, "is Charlotte home?"

"She is, but she's asleep. Come in." He opened the door for Henry and I to enter. "Who's this?"

"My name is Henry," he said, extending his hand.

"Norman," the other man replied, and took it.

"And I'm Timothy," Henry's brother added.

"It's a pleasure to meet you, young man," said Norman.

I leaned closer to Norman, lowering my voice so I wouldn't wake my sleeping sister. "Would you mind if we stay the night?"

"Our door is always open to you, Lillian." We walked inside and paused in the living room. "Timothy, you can sleep down here." He walked over to a linen closet and pulled out an extra blanket. "A sofa fit for a king," he said, gesturing to their small sitting room. Timothy took the blanket and thanked the man, kicking off his ratty old shoes and taking a seat.

Norman led us to the second floor. My sister's beautiful paintings hung on all four walls and I felt as if I had finally arrived at home; a safe, warm home. "I hope this will suffice," Norman said.

There was just one double bed in the room. Henry and I exchanged glances. Norman cleared his throat as we did so. "And, Henry, if you could follow me, there's a second guest room around the corner." He turned back to me as he ushered Henry out the door. "I'll let Charlotte know you're here. She might want to speak with you."

I nodded, too exhausted to argue. "Okay. Goodnight."

Norman laughed. "Goodnight. We'll sort things out in the morning."

"Thank you," I said. Norman left the room. Henry shot a longing look over his shoulder to me before Norman pulled the door shut between us.

Barely a few minutes had passed before a knock came at the door. "Come in," I said, rising from the edge of the bed where I had been sitting.

"Lily," Charlotte breathed, rushing towards me and pulling me in for a long, loving hug. "Father hit you again." Her voice was a concerned whisper as she examined the purple bruise on my face.

"I'm alright, now," I assured her. "I'm with you."

"Good," she replied. "I want you to know that you can stay here with us as long as you need. Father doesn't even need to know. You need to be safe, that's what's most important."

"Ben knows I'm here," I explained. "But I think he'll stay quiet."

"He always has," Charlotte observed. She stood and wandered over to a dresser, pulling out an old nightgown. "I keep some extra clothes in here," she told me. "Just in case."

"Thank you," I said, taking it in my hands.

She cleared her throat and put her hand on the doorknob. "I'll see you tomorrow," she told me.

I couldn't stop the tears from filling my eyes. "Thank you for everything, Charlotte. I… I don't know-"

"I'll always be here for you, Lily," she said, emotion heavy in her voice. "Always. But go to sleep now, okay? You're safe."

I listened to her, changing into the nightgown and tucking myself into the warm sheets of Charlotte's bed, feeling somewhat relaxed for the first time in years. Still, I felt that something was missing. I looked at the untouched pillows beside me, wishing Henry was laying on them. I imagined running my hands through his hair while he slept, curling up close to the heat of his body, tracing lazy circles across his chest as it rose and fell with deep, sleepy breaths.

As if on cue, a knock came at the door and he appeared in the doorway. "Henry!" I lowered my voice to an excited whisper. “What are you doing, I thought Norman-”

“Shh,” he said, approaching me. “What Norman doesn’t know won’t hurt him.” He closed the door quietly behind him and sat down beside me in the bed. “You’re sure you’re alright?” he asked, indicating my bruise.

I nodded. “I am now,” I breathed, and he leaned towards me. The brush of his kiss was soft and easy, laced with longing but held by gentle restraint, no doubt for fear he’d hurt my damaged face.

I didn’t realize how tired I was until we laid down in the bed that night, tucked in each other’s arms. Finally, I could sleep soundly. Finally, I had made it to my destination.

The next morning, we both awoke feeling more rejuvenated than we had in a long time. When we went downstairs together that morning, Charlotte was already standing over the stove, cooking breakfast. She noticed Henry and I walking in together, hand in hand. I half-expected her to say something about it, but she just gave me a knowing smile. “Good morning!” She wiped her hands on her apron and rushed around the counter to give me a tight hug.

She took a step back. "Are you going to introduce me to your traveling companion, here?" she asked, giving me a playful nudge.

"Charlotte, this is Henry," I explained.

"Thank you so much for allowing my brother and I into your home," he said. He offered a handshake, but Charlotte pulled him in for a hug, too.

"Oh, you two just make such a lovely couple," she said. She took my hands and smiled sympathetically. "I'm so glad you're here now," she told me quietly, reinforcing our exchange from the previous night.

"I am too," I said, teary-eyed, and hugged my sister again.

We had breakfast in Charlotte's little kitchen, and then she took us into her bedroom to give us fresh clothing. Timothy remained asleep on the couch for a few more hours. She handed Henry one of Norman's light blue button-down shirts and gave me an extra dress.

The two of us went back to the guest room to get changed. I tried to keep my eyes averted as Henry removed his old white shirt, replacing it with the much larger blue one, but it proved a difficult task. I started laughing as he put it on, realizing that Norman's robust figure was at least two sizes too big for Henry's leaner frame.

"What's so funny?" he asked.

"Nothing," I said, tying the dress my sister had let me borrow and trying not to stare at the excess of material hanging off Henry's torso.

He looked at me with a mischievous grin. "Are you sure about that?"

I nodded, still giggling, and Henry rushed towards me, his shirt still unbuttoned, silencing my laughter with a well-placed kiss. He twirled me through the air of the dusty guest room and we landed on the bed beside each other, hand in hand. I could hear music coming from downstairs.

"Do you hear that?"

"Violin," Henry observed.

We headed downstairs to see Charlotte playing her violin and young Timothy sitting on the edge of the sofa, watching intently. "Henry, come listen! She mentioned that she played and, well, I just had to get a taste," Timothy explained. "Isn't she wonderful?"

Henry joined his brother on the sofa, listening to Charlotte's melody. "Impressive," he said.

"Thank you," Charlotte said. She put down the violin and I noticed the beautiful ring adorning her left hand, glinting in the sunlight. "Lillian mentioned you're a musician?"

He nodded. "I'm a pianist," he explained. "I've always wanted to make a career of it, but it's proving to be a bit difficult."

"He's unbelievably talented," I added, earning myself a smile and a kiss on the cheek from Henry.

"I'm sure he is," Charlotte said, and, after a pause, she turned to Henry's brother. "Now that you're up, Timothy, why don't we get you into some fresh clothes?"

She led him off towards the bedroom and Henry and I were alone once more. "Your sister is remarkably kind," he said quietly.

I joined him on the sofa. "She is. She's a wonderful sister."

He nodded and looked at his feet, a sudden silence falling over the empty room. Henry sucked in a breath. "My brother and I have only two shirts each, you know." His voice broke and he ran a hand through his hair, avoiding my eyes.

Again, my heart fell to the floor. "Henry, I'm so sorry, I…"

"It's okay," he continued. "It's all we've ever known. Our mother passed a long time ago, and our father left us alone on Sixth Avenue when I was just seventeen and Timothy was ten." He took another deep breath and looked at me, eyes glistening. "Charlotte will never know how much she's helping." He paused, collecting himself. "He's everything I have."

"He's safe now." I put a comforting hand on his shoulder. "You're safe now."

"We all are," he said softly. He pulled me into his arms. "I love you, Lillian Abbott," he whispered in my ear, the warmth of his breath sending shivers to my very toes.

"I love you, too."

27

Charlie

Bucksport, Maine, 1990

I walked up the long, winding pathway to Cedar's family home, surrounded by the members of Jonah's band, wondering what exactly possessed me to agree to spend Thanksgiving with all of them. Jonah took my hand, entwining his fingers in my own and I remembered. I was here for him.

A rather plump, middle-aged blonde woman opened the door, wearing a green oven mitt on one hand and holding a wooden spoon in the other. She wore a brightly colored patchwork-style apron reading *I Love My Kids (all five of them)*. It looked to me as if she had sown the product together herself. "Walter!" she cried, making her way down the staircase and towards the group.

I gave Jonah a puzzled look. “Walter?” I mouthed.

He smiled at me and mouthed “just wait,” in response.

The woman grabbed Cedar and frantically pulled him in for a hug. “I missed you so much, Walter,” she said, tears of joy filling her eyes.

“Mom, you have to stop calling me that,” he said through gritted teeth.

“Calling you *Walter*?” she asked, her voice sweet and silvery.

“Yes!”

“Sweetheart, you can’t just throw out your great-grandfather’s name because you think the name of a *tree* sounds cooler,” she said calmly. “Now come in, you guys, dinner will be ready soon.”

“Cedar *is* cooler than Walter,” he muttered under his breath as they headed towards the door.

“I heard that.” She pointed the wooden spoon at him critically, then opened the door for us to enter, smacking her son on the rear with the utensil as he crossed the threshold.

“Mom!”

She laughed. "And who do we have here?" she asked as I entered the home, immediately greeted by the inviting scent of pumpkins and cinnamon.

"I'm Charlie," I said, continuing to look around. A light blue couch with a knitted white throw faced a boxy television, where a bald man, Cedar's father, I assumed, sat with his feet propped up on an oak coffee table. The walls were lined with images of lighthouses from around Maine.

"I'm Debra," she responded. "Walter's mama." She sized up the five boys as we were setting our bags down on the lower landing of her carpeted staircase. "And which one of these hooligans do you belong to?"

"That would be me," Jonah said, stepping forward.

"I was hoping so," said Debra. She took a step towards him, winked, and whispered, "don't tell the others, but you always were my favorite."

Cedar cleared his throat loudly.

"Oh, hush," she chided. She started towards the kitchen and called her family. "Walter's home, everyone!"

Multiple sets of footsteps pounded in all different directions. A little girl appeared first, flying down the staircase at a breakneck speed. "Walter!" she shouted excitedly. She couldn't have been more than five.

A smile broke onto his face as he lifted the little girl into his arms. "Hey there, Daisy," he said to her. "How's your Thanksgiving going?"

"Great!" she replied, her voice high pitched and beyond adorable. She played with a fistful of his red hair and continued. "When are you bringing Maddy back here?"

His smile turned sour and he put her down. "Hopefully soon," he said. "I'm doing my best." I remembered the song Cedar had performed for the residents of Aspen Hall on one my first nights there, suddenly making the connection between the song, the band's name, and the ex-girlfriend. I felt bad for the lovesick singer.

"Hey, Declan."

The honeyed voice belonged to a girl of about seventeen, standing at the end of the hallway. She wore a tight-fitting dress and high heels, and she had even curled her long blonde hair for the holiday. *Or,* I thought, *for Declan.*

Declan's blue eyes widened, and his jaw dropped nearly to the floor when he saw the girl. "Uh, hey, Natalie," he responded, running a nervous hand through his hair.

Cedar approached his bandmate from behind. "Dude, if you so much as *look* at my sister," he threatened, "I will chop you to pieces with my mom's meat cleaver."

I became suddenly aware of the loud chopping sounds coming from the kitchen.

"You haven't changed a bit since last year," Natalie said sweetly, strutting towards him and running one well-manicured finger across his razor-sharp jawline.

He let out a quiet groan, then cleared his throat and turned away. "You, uh, have," he replied.

I squeezed Jonah's hand and kissed him on the cheek. "I'll be right back." I headed into the kitchen where Debra was putting the finishing touches on the meal. "Hey, Debra," I said.

"Hello, Dear." She looked up her bowl of half-mashed potatoes. "What can I do for you?"

"I was wondering if you had a phone I could use, to call my family."

She nodded and rubbed her hands on her apron. "Oh, of course," she said, scurrying through the kitchen and into the dining room.

I followed, and she handed me the phone, attached to a wall adjacent to the table. "Thank you," I said to her, then dialed.

"Hello?"

"Dad?"

"Charlie!" A tone of bitter excitement lined his deep voice. "It's so great to hear from you, happy Thanksgiving!"

"Happy Thanksgiving," I replied. "Is Mom there?"

"She's just finishing up dinner now," he said. "Let me put you on with Grandma."

"Grandma's there?"

"Oh," he continued. "Yes. She… I'll let you talk to her." His voice became distant. "Mom!" he called, "Your granddaughter is on the phone!"

"Charlotte?"

"Hey, Grandma Lily! How's your Thanksgiving?" I asked cheerfully, twirling the black phone cord between my fingers.

"Oh, it's alright," she said. I could sense a hint of dismay in her voice.

"What's the matter, Grandma?"

"It's your grandfather," she replied. "He's not doing so well. His memory's getting worse…" She trailed off.

My heart rate quickened. "What do you mean?" I asked, quickly becoming frantic.

She cleared her throat, obviously struggling to keep it together. "I've had to call the nursing home," she said. "He's… he's not doing very well."

I exhaled slowly, trying my best to keep my cool. "What, um, what does that mean?" I asked.

"It means he won't be living with me anymore," she said. "The two of us are spending Thanksgiving with your dad this year, since he's planning to move out of Adagio, and then Grandpa will go to the nursing home and I will stay in the house."

I sighed. I knew Grandpa's memory was poor, but I didn't realize how bad it had gotten just in the few short weeks I had been at school. I vaguely remembered Dad mentioning that he wanted to move out of Adagio when things started becoming unbearable, but I didn't think it would happen so soon. "I'm so sorry, Grandma," I said to her. "Try to make the best of today, okay?" I paused, my eyes welling up with tears. "Could you put him on for me?"

"Of course, Dear," she said. "I love you."

"I love you too." There was a momentary pause and I heard muffled voices as she handed the phone to my grandfather.

"Hello?"

"Grandpa Henry," I said. "It's Charlie."

He was quiet for a while. "Who?"

I took a deep breath, trying to remind myself that he still loved me, that it wasn't my fault I was slipping from his memory. "Charlotte," I explained. "It's Charlotte."

"Charlotte passed away years ago," he insisted. He sounded weaker than I remembered.

I bit my lip. "No, your granddaughter. Charlie."

He said nothing.

"I just wanted to say I love you, Grandpa," I said. "and I want you to have a great Thanksgiving."

"You too," he said, and hung up the phone.

"Okay, guys," Debra called from the kitchen. "Dinner's ready, wash up!"

I tried to pull myself together for the dinner. I fooled everyone but Jonah, who kept a protective hand on my leg for the entirety, reminding me that he was on my side, that amidst all the chaos, he would be my constant.

28

Lillian

Outskirts of Adagio, Maine, 1934

Nearly a full week had passed since Henry and I first arrived at Charlotte's house. I received a letter from Ben in that time. He wrote to tell me that my siblings were just fine, that Robert was adjusting to working with Father and Samuel had been doing well in school. He calmed my worries about Mary, telling me that she was perfectly safe, and he would continue to protect her with everything he had.

Just a few days after I had received that first letter from Ben, Charlotte asked me to fetch the mail while she finished fixing up our lunch. I obliged, putting on a long overcoat and heading out the front door, down the winding dirt path and to her little mailbox. I flicked through the letters as I returned to the house.

"Charlotte, did you write back to Ben yet?"

"No, why?" She removed her oven mitts and exited the kitchen, meeting me near the door and looking over my shoulder at the letter I held in my hands, addressed to both of us.

"Nor did I," I replied. "I wonder why he's written again so soon."

"I don't know," she said. "We'll just have to open it."

I agreed and took the letter to the dining table where we tore it open and examined its contents. Charlotte began reading first. "'Dear Sisters,' he wrote, 'I apologize for writing you again after just two days, but I fear this matter requires your urgent attention…" She put a hand to her mouth and her eyes welled with tears.

"What's wrong?" I asked. "What does the letter say?"

She handed it to me and returned to the kitchen, saying nothing. Concerned, I unfolded the letter and began to read it to myself,

Dear Sisters,

I apologize for writing you again after just two days, but, unfortunately, this matter requires your

urgent attention. I would have told you in my previous letter, but this problem has only recently come to light. I fear Mary has struck ill. She has been weak, feverish, and has not left her bed. I've written to the doctor, but he has been away and still has not yet written back. For now, I am doing all I can with my own knowledge and equipment. It is a danger, though, as I am afraid that she may have caught influenza. Write back immediately, sisters. If the worst is to happen, Mary will need both of you here, at home.

Lillian, I know you have only just left us, but I beg now for your return. I hope you can face Father in order to help us care for Mary, and to say goodbye, if the worst happens. I know it will be difficult, but we must all be strong now for Mary's sake.

Charlotte, we haven't seen you in months. While I am very glad you are happy and safe with Norman, I think it imperative that you now come back to see us and to see your youngest sister. Give Norman my regards.

I love you both so very much. I ask that you write back soon and let me know if you'll be seeing us shortly. Please be punctual. I fear our sister doesn't have much time.

With Love,

Ben

I sat there for a moment, frozen, holding the paper in my shaking hands.

The front door swung open and Henry appeared. I couldn't pull my eyes away from Ben's writing. I simply sat there and called him over.

"What's wrong?" he asked.

I gathered the strength to stand tucked myself into his arms, weeping softly. "Mary's fallen ill," I said quietly.

"Lillian, I'm so sorry." He kissed the top of my head and rubbed my back.

I stepped away from him, drying my eyes and tucking my hair back behind my ears. I took a deep breath, trying to calm myself down. "It's okay," I said. "I'll be right back.

I stepped around him and headed into the kitchen where Charlotte had gone when she first read the letter. I didn't see her right away. "Charlotte?"

"Back here," she said, sounding weak and labored.

I went to the source of the sound, finding Charlotte tucked behind her kitchen counter, crying. I sat myself right next to her and put an arm around her. "When do you want to go?"

She gulped. "I don't know," she said with a sniffle. "I…"

"You're not considering staying here?"

She looked at me, her face red and blotchy, raw emotion in her eyes. "I don't know if I can go back, Lily," she said. "I'm scared."

I pulled my sister close to me. "I know," I said to her. "I am too. But we have to go back for Mary." I paused. "We're stronger together, Charlotte. He can't get to the both of us, not if we stand together."

"You're right. We have to be there for her, no matter what…no matter *who* we must face." She nodded and squeezed my hand. "Thank you," she said, still teary-eyed.

"I love you," I told her.

"I love you too, Lily." She stood up and helped me to my feet. "We'll leave first thing tomorrow."

"Okay," I said, and followed her through the kitchen. "Charlotte."

She turned to me, wiping the last of the tears from her face. "Yes?"

"What…do…do you think she'll make it?"

Charlotte nodded. "She's *our* sister," she said. "If she's anything, she's resilient. She'll make it through this, I'm sure of it."

The rest of the day was a blur. Charlotte explained her plans to Norman, told him that if she didn't return by Monday to send for her. I took comfort in Henry's arms and he tried to lighten the mood by playing the rickety, out of tune piano Charlotte kept in the sitting room. Somehow, he still managed to make even the most damaged of instruments sound like music from the heavens. I laughed and watched Timothy as he danced ridiculously to his brother's upbeat melodies.

Later that night, I found that sleep evaded me. I thought of all of the troubles my little sister must have been going through at that moment in time. Was she resting peacefully in her bed? Was she scared, alone in her room, wishing I was by her side? Was she feeling ill, her small body slowly declining and giving in to the perils of sickness?

I rolled over, wishing sleep would come. I watched Henry's chest rise and fall, the rhythmic beat of his heart seeming to be the only constant. Still, ruinous thoughts plagued my mind. I couldn't help but wonder if my running away was, somehow, a catalyst for this tragic turn of events. What if Mary's falling ill was a message from God, a message telling me I should never abandon my family?

What if I had made the wrong choice?

29

Charlie

Pine Ridge University, 1990

The call I made to home on Thanksgiving rattled me to my core. No matter how I tried to shake my worry, my thoughts always returned to my grandfather's declining state. The next few days, I existed in a fog. The world around me continued to spin, but I was stuck in my own head. Jonah helped. But I still felt lost.

It was the weekend before finals. Jonah, Shane and I were in the library, piles of books, papers and note sheets galore stacked all around us. I sat on the floor, looking intently at a book detailing the history of the Baroque era. I stared at the pages, the lines of words, the black and white photographs, the example lines of sheet music. None of it sunk in. My mind was elsewhere.

"Charlie?"

I jumped and looked up. Shane was standing over me, trying to get my attention. Jonah knelt behind him, picking up stacks of books and returning them to their places on their respective shelves. "Yeah, sorry," I said, rubbing my aching temples. "What?"

"Are you ready to go?"

"Uh, yeah," I said. "You go on ahead, I'll catch up in a second."

Shane disappeared through the rows of shelves and started downstairs. I inhaled deeply, the smell of dust and old, dry-rotting book bindings invading my nostrils. I leaned back against the wall, holding my head in my hands. *Pull yourself together*, I scolded myself. *Grandpa's not gone. Not yet.*

Jonah's hand appeared before me and I snapped back to reality. I took it and he helped me to my feet. He hugged me from behind, resting his head on my shoulder. "It's gonna be okay, you know," he reminded me. "You're gonna get through this. You're strong." He kissed my neck. "Let's go."

I slung my yellow nylon backpack over one shoulder and tugged on my knit beanie. We walked off towards the doors, through a seemingly endless maze of books. When we arrived outside, the cold bit at my fingertips and nose. The nighttime air had grown even colder, and I pulled my hands into the sleeves of my jacket as silent snowflakes fell into my hair.

"Jonah?" I asked, my eyes meeting his as we walked towards my residence hall, red brick buildings and lampposts casting shadows of snow flurries lining the pathways.

"Hmm?"

"Thank you," I said.

"What for?" he asked, perplexed.

I struggled to find the words. I was no poet. "For making me… A better version of myself," I replied.

He let out a slight laugh. "Oh, Charlie," he said.

"What?"

"I don't make you better. You were always perfect."

We stopped. The snow started to lay on the pathways around us. "No, I mean…"

He took my hands again, gazing at me intently. "I know what you mean. And I'm telling you. The Charlie standing in front of me? She's always been there. She was just… A little shy."

I blushed, watching his eyes wander down to my lips. He kissed me softly, his lips a burst of warmth against the freezing temperatures. I could see his breath as he pulled away from me just enough to speak and whispered, "she still overthinks things too much, though."

"Hey!" I laughed and playfully punched his shoulder through his thick winter jacket.

He stepped back, a naughty smile appearing on his face. He let out this ridiculous laugh and lunged towards me, catching me in his arms before I even had the chance to escape. I doubled over in laughter, his grip tickling my sides. I struggled for a moment, trying to gain some sort of leverage, but he managed to turn me all the way around, so we ended up facing each other. Both of our expressions softened as I threw my arms around his neck and dove in for a kiss.

We eventually let go of each other and returned to our respective dorms, mentally preparing for finals to start in just a few short days. I tossed about in my bed that night, trying to relax to the point of sleep. *She still overthinks things too much, though,* Jonah's voice echoed through my mind.

He was right. But I was still going to continue to overthink. When my alarm clock read 2:45 a.m. and I still hadn't fallen asleep, I got up and pulled on a pair of sweatpants, heading down to the common room. There was a payphone in the bottom floor of Aspen Hall for residents to use. To my relief, no one was in the common room when the elevator opened up.

I shuffled over and popped a quarter in the machine.

"Hello?" my mother croaked.

"Did I wake you?"

"No, Sweetheart, it's okay. What's wrong?"

"I'm just… I'm thinking about Grandpa. Is he okay?"

My mother said nothing. She let out a sigh. "Look, Charlie, we were planning on calling the school tomorrow about this…"

"What is it?" I demanded, my worries beginning to boil over.

"He's not doing well, Charlie," she said, her voice cracking. "He's had a heart attack, and, well, your father's inconsolable."

"What do you mean, 'he's not doing well?'" I cried. "He can't die, don't tell me he's gonna die!"

An RA walked past me and gave me a critical look. "Quiet hours," he mouthed.

I ignored him.

"We don't know what's going to happen," said my mother on the other end. "But… we do want you to come home. To see him. Just in case."

I nodded, swallowing back my tears. "Okay. I'll leave now."

"No," she said immediately. "It's too late, you're upset. Wait until tomorrow."

"Mom, I can't-"

"Charlie." Her voice was sharp and demanding, her fierceness cutting through the phone line.

"Okay," I conceded, knowing that driving in the dark, snow-covered night wouldn't be the smartest thing to do in my current emotional state. "I'll see you in the morning. Love you, Mom." I hung up the phone and hurried back up to my room, turning the key in the lock as gently as possible, worried I'd wake up Ruby. I climbed into bed, hoping to get at least a bit of sleep before I would embark on my journey.

After a fitful night of sleep, I awoke early. Ruby still slept soundly in her bed, so I scribbled a note and left it on her desk, giving her my parents' phone number and telling her I'd be gone for a few days. I grabbed my backpack and my car keys, hoping I had enough clothing in my dresser at home to last for at least the rest of the week.

The rubber toe of my sneaker hit the edge of my desk as I tried my best to maneuver my way out of the dark room. It took all the strength I could muster not to curse.

Ruby grunted and, despite my frantic prayers that she would just roll over and go back to sleep, she flicked on her bedside lamp and glared at me.

"Ruby, I'm so sorry for waking you," I said. "I just really need to get home now, and I..."

She put a hand to her forehead and sat up. "What the hell?"

"Look, I'm sorry," I said. "There's just some family stuff going on, and..."

She interrupted me again, waving her hand about and making a noise. "No, no I don't care that you woke me," she said.

"Good, thanks," I said, picking up my dropped backpack from the floor. "I'll just leave then."

"Wait." There was undeniable anger in her voice as she rose from the bed and moved across the dark room towards me. Somehow, she still managed to look perfect, even right after this surprise awakening. I couldn't help but be a little angered by it. "Why didn't you tell me?"

"Tell you what?" I had a sinking suspicion that I knew exactly what she was going to say.

"That you're banging Jonah."

"Ruby, it's not..."

Her expression was growing more and more frantic as she advanced towards me. "I thought you cared about me, I thought you knew I have a huge crush on him!"

"Okay, first of all," I began, "We're not just *banging*. I really care about him."

Ruby rolled her eyes and scoffed, "Oh, *please*." Her voice was venomous. "I've talked to him before. He's just a regular, boring boy with an extremely pretty face and incredible abs."

I could feel the heat of anger in my chest. I clenched my jaw and tried my best to be calm with her. "Look, Ruby, I'm really sorry I didn't tell you..."

"You should be!" She paused. "I thought I could trust you. I thought we would be friends. I guess I was wrong."

I ran a hand through my auburn hair and rubbed my throbbing temples. "I'm sorry, I really am, I just have a lot going on right now."

"Yeah, you always do," she said, turning around and climbing back into her bed. She ran a hand through her hair "Go," she said. "You obviously can't stand to spend another minute here with me."

"It's not like that, I..."

"Just go."

I did. I just went. My stomach hurt when I thought about Ruby and the damage I had done to our relationship, but it hurt more when I thought about my grandpa and his declining health.

"You can do this," I muttered to myself as I started the engine. The drive was long and exhausting, and for the majority of the time my mind was elsewhere. I didn't even remember getting off the highway and entering my sequestered little seaside town, but before I knew it, I was pulling into my parents' driveway.

I leaned against my steering wheel and exhaled, the sight of my own home seeming somehow strange to me after spending so many weeks living in a dorm. Opening the car door, I was greeted by the calming sound of the ocean waves, a warm and welcome reminder of home.

"I'm home," I said, pushing open the back door and entering the house. The first vision to meet my eyes was my mother, sitting in our old rocking chair, book in hand, anxiously awaiting my arrival. Her once-brilliant red hair had started graying, her brown eyes seemed to have lost some of their youthful glow, and stress and age had begun to draw wrinkles on her face. To me, she was still as beautiful as ever.

My mother rushed towards me, enveloping me in the warmth of her loving arms. “Hi, Baby,” she said.

“Where’s Dad?”

“He’s upstairs,” my mother replied.

I headed up the stairs to see my father, wanting nothing more than to see him, to hug him, to tell him that I loved him. When I arrived at the top of the stairs, I could see the light radiating from the gap at the bottom of my parents’ bedroom door.

I raised my fist, but I couldn’t bring myself to knock. Hearing my dad’s sobs through the wooden-paneled door was too much for me. He was the strongest man I knew, and just past that door he sat, breaking to pieces.

30

Lillian

Outskirts of Adagio, Maine, 1934

I tried not to shake as I guided the pen along the page, the blotches of ink forming into words I never thought I'd write:

Charlotte –

I know we had planned to go back together. But I want to be strong for you. I know you're having a tough time coming to terms with our sudden return to Father, and I don't want to force you to go if you're too scared. I'm leaving tonight. I'll see you soon. Please make sure Henry and Timothy are safe. I don't think I'll be seeing them for a while. I have to do what's best for him, for you, for Mary.

You need to stay here with Norman. Stay safe. I love you.

Lily

I left the note on the dining room table, right next to where Ben's letter still sat. Leaning against the table, I let doubts creep back into my mind.

No.

It was selfish to think of staying. Going back there, alone, would be best for everyone. I had no other choice.

I looked at Henry's lantern resting in my shaking fingers, and, for a moment, I thought maybe I should leave it behind. I shook my head, deciding it was too dangerous to go out so late at night without it. Besides, it would be something to remember him by, if the worse would happen.

I took my jacket off the hook and headed out into the darkness, hoping no one would hear me sneaking out. I couldn't bear the thought of Mary at home, scared, sick. I had to be there with her, and I couldn't rest until I was.

I trudged along the rocky Maine coastline, heading north towards my father's estate. Thunder crashed and I gasped, watching lightning strike the ocean in the horizon. I shivered. I hadn't realized the weather would be fighting me so.

Still, I trekked on. It pained my heart to think of Henry, to think of how I left him behind, but alone in my contemplation I had realized there was no other choice. Running away with him had created an irreparable rift, I couldn't damage what little relationship I had left with my family by making another mistake. Waves crashed against the coast as I pushed against the wind, praying for safety, praying I would make it back home.

I wiped the tears from my eyes, unable to bear the thought that just a week prior, I had been saying the same prayer, in the hopes Henry and I would make it safely to Charlotte's.

But I had given up.

"Lillian!" He shouted over the roar of the storm. "Lillian, stop!"

Clouds shaded the moonlight and rain poured. I turned around and raised the lantern. "Henry, what are you doing out here?" I yelled, "It's not safe!"

He approached me. "Lillian, what are *you* doing? Why leave us now? Why put yourself in danger? Charlotte was preparing for you to leave in the morning! Together!"

"I made a mistake, Henry!" My tears mixed with the thundering rain. I pushed a wet strand of hair out of my face. "I shouldn't have left my family!"

"What are you saying?"

I shook my head. "You have to let me go," I said. I touched his shoulder, where Norman's shirt now clung to his skin from the pouring rain. "I'm sorry." I turned around and started back down the coastline.

He grabbed my hand and pulled me back around, kissing me with more force than he ever had before. I wished I hadn't enjoyed it quite so much.

"No," he said softly.

I pushed him away. "Yes," I said, worrying that he could hear the pain in my voice.

He shook his head and approached me again. "No, Lillian. I'll never let you go. I care too much for you."

"Henry, I can't pull you into this. It's not your fault, it's mine. I have to go fix what I've destroyed with my family."

"You don't understand!" he cried. "Maybe it's selfish of me to want you all to myself. Maybe I'm a horrible person for wanting you to stay here with me. Maybe I'm not a dream come true for you, but Lillian... I can't imagine what life would be like without you."

I just let the rain beat down on me, soaking through my hair, my dress, my skin. I watched as Henry did the same, begging me with his eyes.

"I love you! I love you more than I can even fathom, Lillian."

"Henry, you…"

"It's terrifying. I know it's scary for you, but I'm terrified, too. I didn't know I could love someone like I love you. I didn't know that I could be so in love with someone that the thought of being away from you..." He broke off, collecting himself, then moved closer to me, until our faces were mere inches from each other. "I know you. I know all of you, Lily, inside and out. I know that you love those tiny blue wildflowers that grow in the grass outside your sister's cottage. I know that you have a little freckle on top of your right wrist. I know that you have an adventurous spirit, that if you hadn't been forced to spend your days in that house, you'd be out gallivanting in the mountains. I know that you're more passionate about your siblings than anything in the world, that you'd give your life for them in an instant." He paused. "I know you love me, Lillian. And I know you're scared." He slipped his hands behind my ears and pressed his forehead against mine while rain slid down both of our faces. "But I'm with you, and I don't plan on leaving you behind anytime soon."

"I do love you, Henry," I replied, biting my lip and stepping away. "And I always will." Henry's hands fell to his sides and I wiped the tears from my face, taking a deep breath. "But I have to do this alone." I turned and continued walking, leaving him behind.

"Lillian!" he called, the emotion in his voice ringing through the clamor of the storm.

I turned. "Goodbye, Henry," I said, tears now streaming down my face. I didn't know what else to do. Maybe someday we could be together again. But at that moment, it seemed he was too far out of reach. The absolute anguish of his absence burdened my heart, but still I knew that I had to do what was right for my siblings.

I had to stay strong for Mary. I refused to let my feelings for Henry get in the way of her health, her safety, her life. She had to come first.

I arrived at my father's house not long after, feet aching with exhaustion as I climbed those steps yet again. I sized the door up and down. Had it always looked so menacing?

The door swung open with one quick push and once again, I was back in the grips of my family home. I leaned my back against the wall just outside of Mary's room and slid down, the hardwood floor panels cold against the backs of my legs.

The white door swung open beside me. "Lillian?"

I rose to my feet and hugged my brother. "Hi, Ben," I said.

"Did you just get here? Are you alone? Where's Charlotte? Henry?"

Tears burned my eyes at the mention of his name. "Yes," I said. "I'll explain everything. I'm here now, that's what matters."

"You're soaked," he observed. "Did you walk all the way here in the storm?"

I nodded.

"Come on," he said. "Let's get you cleaned up, and I'll make some tea."

31

Charlie

Adagio Hills Hospital, 1990

The rhythmic beeping of machines surrounded me as I stood in that white room, staring at Grandpa lying coldly in that bed, the hospital gown hanging loose on his frail body, tubes tangled in a web all over his body. Grandma Lily sat beside him, folding her hands around his and humming softly a melody I didn't recognize.

His eyes fluttered open at the sound of her voice and he gave a labored smile. I stood there quietly, just observing. I knew trying to talk to him would just upset him, but I had to see for myself that he was alive.

I thought of my own father in that moment. I thought about the way he cried in his room, while I sat just outside the door. I thought of the lost expression on his face when he opened the door and saw me sitting there, curled in a ball on the carpet.

"What are you doing out here?" He had asked. I knew he was trying to sound brave, but I could hear the crackling tension in his voice, I could see the worry on his face, the gray in his hair, the stress he was under.

I couldn't think of the words to reply to him. He led me into his room, and we sat together on the edge of his bed. No words came to me to describe how the both of us felt, so I muttered a quiet, "I'm sorry."

"Don't be," he had told me, standing and moving towards the dresser, where a picture of my grandfather rested in a small silver frame. "He was an amazing father, you know."

"*Is*," I had corrected.

My father nodded. "You're right," he had replied, returning to the bed. He continued to tell me more stories than I could count. He told me of learning to ride a bike, Grandpa Henry steadying him. He described the hours they had spent at a piano, Grandpa explaining chords but my dad just not quite understanding. He explained Grandpa's constant support, his balanced discipline, his unwavering love.

I thought about those stories then, as I looked at the tubes and wires and listened to the incessant beeping. I watched his chest rise and fall with each labored breath; glad my father had told me those stories. I wished only that I could go back in time and see Grandpa Henry in his prime.

My mother appeared at the door. "Charlie?" she called in softly.

I looked over at her.

"It's time for us to go," she said.

I nodded in agreement, not wanting to keep my father at the hospital any longer than necessary. I knew it was terribly hard for him to watch his hero, the man who raised him, crumble and deteriorate before his eyes. I gave Grandma a kiss on the cheek and headed out into the hallway, leaving my grandparents alone.

I followed my parents out through the sliding glass doors of Adagio Hills Hospital and into the expansive parking lot. My dad didn't shed a tear the whole time, but the lines on his face told another tale.

"We're going to move out of Adagio," he told me as he started the car.

I wanted to argue, but I was simply too drained. I said nothing.

The car ride home was brief and quiet. I just sat there, staring out the window, watching the evening snow begin to stick to the grass and sidewalks. We arrived at home to a ringing phone. While my mom answered it, I plopped down on the couch, absorbing the warmth of familiarity. Leaning back, I could feel the itchy material of my mother's hand-knit blanket thrown on the back of the couch. The little TV sat on an oaken end table. I smiled when I looked at it, remembering the day Dad and Grandpa built it out of scrap wood from my grandmother's old dresser. *To new beginnings,* they had said. *Out with the old memories, in with the new.* I didn't quite understand why they would tear down such a beautiful dresser rather than just fix the few dents and splinters in the wood, but I figured it was a nice sentiment all the same.

"Hello?" my mom said. She covered it with one hand and turned to me. "It's a boy named Shane," she whispered. "He says it's important."

I rolled my eyes and moved lazily over to her. "Hello?" I said, my tone weary and resigned.

"Charlie, it's Shane." I sighed.

"What do you want, Shane?"

"Whoa, sorry," he said.

"Ugh, no," I replied. "You didn't do anything. It's just been a stressful day. Go ahead."

"Sorry, Charlie," he repeated. "But, uh, could you put Jonah on really quick?"

"What?" I glanced quickly around my house, as if I wasn't completely sure that I hadn't brought Jonah home with me.

"Just give him the phone."

"Shane, what are you talking about?"

I listened for his response, but I heard only the slightest crackle of static coming from the phone line.

"Shane?" I repeated.

"He's not there?"

My heart rate quickened. Was something wrong? Was he okay? "No, he's not here," I said. "What do you mean?"

"Shit."

"Shane! What's going on?"

"Earlier today, we were all gonna go get ice cream at Donny's," he said. "Jonah knocked on your door and your roommate got mad and said you went home, and he got all worried. He tried to call, but you guys must have been out. He couldn't think of anything else, so he went after you. I just thought he'd be there by now."

My heart dropped. I hoped he had just gotten lost on his way into Adagio. The town was small, just a tiny little speck compared to the bigger cities in Maine. "Wh…What are you saying, Shane? He's out there somewhere?"

"He left five hours ago."

"Adagio is only two hours from school," I replied, suddenly terrified of what I had done. Why hadn't I thought to tell Jonah I was leaving? This whole ordeal was all my fault.

I could tell Shane was getting nervous. "Charlie, go find him. You've got to go find him."

I nodded, not that Shane could see me all the way from school. "Yes," I said. "I'm leaving right now." I hung up the phone and grabbed my keys. "I'm going out," I called to my mom.

"Okay," she said, her voice ringing from upstairs. "Stay safe!"

"I will," I said, rushing out the door. I turned my key in the ignition with shaking hands. *Calm down,* I told myself. *Everything is fine. I'm sure he's fine.*

There was only one way to get in and out of Adagio. Going at least fifteen miles an hour over the speed limit, I rushed in that direction, keeping my eyes peeled for that rickety old Volkswagen. I smiled through a mist of tears as

I remembered the many memories we had made in that car, the countless adventures, all the times Jonah would scold me for playing with the cracking leather of the seats. I remembered the glove box that wouldn't stay shut, the papers that always fell into my lap. I remembered the laughter, the tears, the ups and the downs. I hoped I wasn't headed into the beginning of a terrible memory.

I was only about two miles past the Adagio border when my worst fear was realized. There was his car, sitting just off the side of the road, the front end wrapped around a tree.

I pulled off the road as quickly as I could and put on my flashers, rushing out of the car to see if he was okay. I peered through the passenger side window and saw him sitting in there, Bon Jovi music still playing, though its sound had become muffled, out of tune, and weak.

His head had clearly smashed into the steering wheel, and he leaned against it, his eyes shut and blood caked on the side of his face. I felt an indescribable pit in my stomach, a pain I could never explain, a pain that shook me to my core.

I pounded my fists against the window. "Jonah!" I shouted, panic coursing through my veins.

His eyes opened and he managed to twist himself around in the seat just enough to open the door. I flew around the car and to his side. “Hey, Cutie,” he said to me, tapping my nose as he tumbled out of the car in a heap. His voice was labored, I could tell breathing was becoming more difficult.

“Jonah, what the hell?” I tried to check every inch of him for serious injuries, wishing I knew how to help him. “What were you thinking?”

“I was worried!” he said, bristling with defense.

“You’ve never been reckless like this, Jonah.”

“I’ve never been hopelessly in love with someone who has a habit of disappearing,” he retorted.

I rolled my eyes, hoping he wouldn’t see how much I was blushing. “You’re lucky you’re alive,” I scolded.

“Yeah,” he conceded. “Should’ve remembered to get those brakes checked.”

“You’re such an idiot,” I told him. He gasped, grabbing at his side. “We need to get you to a hospital,” I continued. “Can you walk?”

He nodded. “I think so.” He leaned against me and struggled to his feet, still clutching his injured side.

I managed to get him safely into the car, with just a little difficulty. “Wait,” he said as I tried to shut the door.

“What?”

"My Bon Jovi tapes," he said, gesturing to the wreckage.

I rolled my eyes. "Really?"

"Just go get them," he said. "At least the one with our song on it."

Despite being incredibly annoyed, I couldn't help the butterflies that formed in my stomach at his mention of our song. I hurried back to his car and scrounged through the pile of tapes until I found the right one.

"You okay?" I asked him as I got back in the car.

"I'm fine," he said, wincing. "Do you have it?"

"Here." I handed him the tape and drove off towards the hospital, for the second time that day.

32

Lillian

Adagio, Maine, 1934

I sat by Mary's bedside, watching her little chest rise and fall with each labored breath. She was wrapped up in a soft pink blanket, knit by Mother during the months of her pregnancy. I ran my fingers through my little sister's fine hair, marveling at her beauty.

Her room was dark, quiet, peaceful. I looked around, remembering how I watched her grow up in that very room. Her bed sat in front of the window, and beside it was a very old wooden rocking chair. It was the same chair Mother had used to read stories to each of us at night before bed when we were small, and a million memories came rushing back as I sat there looking at it. A beautiful mirror sat atop her dresser, random knick-knacks and baubles all around it. Mary had given each little trinket a name and a story, from the angel figurine named Dorothy to the goofy circus clown she named after Sammy.

She opened her eyes slowly, her eyelashes fluttering. "Lillian," she said. Although her voice had grown weak with sickness, I could hear how happy she was to see me there beside her.

"Hi there, Mary," I said gently. "How are you feeling?"

She shrugged. "Not great."

I looked up at the sound of a delicate knock on the door and saw Ben step inside. "Hello, girls." A pause. "How are we doing?"

"Best we can, considering," I said with a chuckle.

He nodded and handed Mary a tall glass of water. "Sip it slowly." He turned to me. "I think Mother wanted to see you," he said.

I got up and headed to the door. "I'll see you soon, Mary."

"Lillian, there you are," my mother said, coming towards me. "How's Mary?"

"She's not great, but I think she'll be alright," I replied. "From what I've seen, things are looking up."

"Okay," my mother said, relief in her voice. "Father's just gone to fetch the doctor, just in case."

I nodded. "Does he know I'm home yet?"

"He does. I spoke with him about it this morning before you were awake," Mother told me.

"What did he say?" I asked, noticing my hands suddenly clamming up.

"He's obviously angry you ever left, after the lengths he went to in order to keep you here, however cruel they were," she explained, "but he's glad you decided to come back." Noticing my worried expression, she continued. "I wouldn't worry about him; he's focused entirely on Mary. We're all focused on Mary." She let out a soft cry and held her face in her hands.

I placed a comforting hand on her shoulder. "I think she'll be okay, Mom," I said. "Really."

She gave me a hug. "I'm so glad you came back to us," she told me. "I know it's been hard. You're so strong for coming back." Her tears were hot against my neck.

We walked over to the sitting room, across the beautiful hardwood flooring and sat on the sofa under one of Charlotte's old paintings. "I had to come back. I felt so guilty for running away like I did, I…" I trailed off, and after a moment, collected myself. "There's this boy," I said.

She smiled, but her eyes were glistening. "I know," she said.

"You do?"

"Lillian, you're my daughter," she said. "I knew the day you met him. You didn't have to tell me. I knew something changed. You had met your match."

I blushed. "He's truly wonderful," I said.

"I'm sure he is."

"I know I shouldn't have run off with him," I said again. "I should have considered the consequences..."

My mother took my hand in hers and looked at me softly. "I don't blame you," she insisted. "I'm not upset. I would've done the same thing."

I gave her a puzzled look.

She shifted in her seat and bit her lip, as she always did when she was nervous. "Lillian, I never told you about this before," she said, "but..." she paused and cleared her throat. "Your father..."

"What about him?" I urged.

She looked about the room, as if father was some sort of creature, hiding just beyond the door, waiting for the perfect moment to pounce. "He wasn't my first love, Sweetheart."

"What do you mean?" Of course, I wasn't exactly fond of my father, but to know that my mother wasn't deeply in love with him was a shock, to say the least.

"I mean, I didn't meet your father until I had already tried to run away with someone. His name was Jonathan. He worked in the mines, barely had a penny to his name. I settled for your father when I realized it would be better for my future family." She let out a pitiful laugh, her eyes filling with tears. "How wrong was I?"

I gave her a sympathetic look. "Mom, none of this is your fault," I reminded her. I could still scarcely believe her words.

She shook her head and sighed. "I know, I know," she said. "If I hadn't decided to marry him, I wouldn't have you. I wouldn't have your brothers and sisters."

I grinned.

"But for a long time, before Benjamin came along, I regretted my choice. I wished I hadn't settled. I wanted to go back to Jonathan. What I'm trying to tell you, Lily, is that I don't want you to make the same mistakes I did. Don't settle for anyone or anything other than your greatest love."

“So,” I began, trying to figure out how to ask the question plaguing my mind, “you aren’t staying with Father because you’re in love?”

She shook her head. “No,” she said. “no, I’m afraid your father and I were simply… Convenient.” She wiped away a tear.

“Then why did you?” I had always thought Mother loved Father endlessly, despite his obvious flaws. I thought the reason she stayed with him was because she could see through his fury and know the man behind it all.

“For you,” she said simply, letting out a soft cry. “For you, for Ben, for Charlotte… For Samuel and Mary. I know your father can be difficult, but the truth is, I wouldn’t be able to care for all five of you on my own.”

“Mom, I… I don’t know what to say.”

“Just listen to me, Lily,” she said, putting a comforting arm around me. “I wonder every day what would’ve happened if I hadn’t broken his heart. I don’t want you to have the same regrets.”

A single tear slipped from my eye. “I fear I’ve ruined things, Mother,” I told her. “I angered him when I left. I didn’t want him to come with me.”

“If he truly loves you, he’ll give you another chance,” she said. “I know it.”

We embraced for just a fleeting moment before Ben burst through the doorway. “How much longer until the doctor will arrive?”

Flustered, my mother replied, “Father’s gone to fetch him, they should be here any minute now.” She rushed towards him. “Why, what’s happened?”

He shook his head. “Her fever is incredibly high,” he said. “She’s gotten worse.”

“Well, what should we do?”

“I’ve done everything I can,” he explained. “I need the doctor.” Ben’s expression was one I had never seen. He was always the calmest person in the room, but in that moment, his face was red with worry, with fear he’d lost little Mary. “I… I can’t save her by myself,” he said quietly.

Mother and I tried our best to comfort him, but he shook his head and pushed away our hands. “I’m fine.” He started back towards the staircase. “Come upstairs.”

We followed him back upstairs to see my sister. When we arrived, I gasped, a monstrous scene unfolding before my eyes.

Her body moved in a way I had never seen before; her arms and legs had gone stiff and she shook in a most unsettling manner. Mother and I grabbed hold of each other, both of us unsure of how to react to such a sight. She shouted prayers to the heavens, for fear that her daughter's life hung in the balance.

"Help me hold her down," Ben cried, rushing to her side. "She's having a seizure," he explained as I knelt down beside her, holding onto her writing little body, "they sometimes happen when the fever spikes too high."

The door shot open and I shuddered at the sound of my father's voice. "What's going on?" He bellowed, bolting to Mary's bedside.

"Let me through," the doctor said, following Father inside and pushing Ben and I out of the way.

The whole ordeal lasted no more than six minutes, but they were six minutes from Hell.

And they felt like a whole eternity.

33

Charlie

Adagio Hills Hospital, 1990

"Careful, careful," I said, steadying Jonah with my arm as we hobbled into the emergency room entrance.

When we made it inside, the next few hours were chaotic. Flurries of doctors, nurses, and radiologists did all they could to help Jonah to the best of their abilities. I was beyond stressed, but somehow managed to keep my cool for his sake.

The air in the waiting room was heavy. Groups of people sat there, waiting to be called back, waiting to hear results about sick family members, waiting for either great news or the worst news they'll ever hear. I paced back and forth, having no interest in the green padded seats or the stacks of magazines filling the room. My focus was on one thing: Jonah.

I noticed a payphone just outside the waiting room and I put a few quarters in, deciding it would be best to alert my parents of the situation.

"Hello?"

"Mom, it's Charlie."

"Charlie? Where've you been, are you alright?"

"Yeah," I said, trying not to get choked up. "yeah, I'm okay. Um, my boyfriend was in a car accident, so I'm at the hospital with him right now." My voice cut out and I twirled my fingers in my hair nervously.

"Wait – your what?"

Shit. I had never even told my mother that Jonah and I were dating. I knew she wouldn't like that I had been kissing a boy rather than focusing on my studies. "Um, I have a boyfriend," I repeated nervously.

"Charlie, you *what*?"

"Mom, spare the lecture this time," I begged, "please."

Sensing my distress, she eased the pressure. "Okay," she said. "We'll talk about it later. What do you need?"

"What, um, what am I supposed to do?"

"What do you mean, Sweetheart?"

I fought back tears, a million questions flying about in my head. "Should I call someone? What about his car? Should I try get it towed? I don't know how to tell his dad! What about his insurance? I don't even know if he has insurance!"

"Shh, shh," my mom said. "Calm down. I'll make some calls, don't worry. It'll all be fine. Stay at the hospital, I'm sending your father. He'll be there soon."

"Hasn't Dad gone through enough today?" I asked, worried that my father's selflessness would end up doing him in.

"You're his daughter, Charlie. He would give you the moon, if you asked. He'll be there for you."

A wave of relief eased the nervous pounding of my heart. "Thank you, Mom."

"But, Charlie?" She returned to that ambiguous tone landing somewhere between gentle and critical.

"Yeah?"

"I'm helping because I love you, but don't think you're off the hook. We'll be having a talk later."

"Okay." I hung up the phone and continued to pace back and forth in the waiting room. Remembering what

Jonah had told me just a few days prior, I tried my best not to overthink and worry, but I couldn't help myself. Questions floated through my mind. Are his injuries serious? How long will it take for him to heal? Will he be able to come back to campus for finals?

Will he get better?

It only took about fifteen minutes for my father to arrive in the waiting room. "Sit down," he told me.

Too exhausted to argue, I took a seat. My legs continued to bounce as nervousness pulsated through me. "Dad, I just want to say I'm sorry," I said.

"I know, Charlie. Don't worry about it. Your mother has just been so stressed, I hope you understand, with your grandfather and everything going on…"

I pulled him in for a hug. "I get it, Dad. Mom and I will be fine. But Jonah, he's really been helping me through it."

"You really do like this boy, don't you?" he asked, a cynical smile toying at the edges of her mouth.

I nodded. "Very much."

"Look, Charlie, I know your mom and I have been hard on you about focusing on your studies, but you *are* an adult now-"

"I am."

"Don't push it."

"Sorry."

"Anyway, you're technically an adult. You're in college, you have to learn these things and prioritize on your own. I get it. And I think your mother does too. It's just hard for her to let go," he said.

I looked at him and smiled. "Thanks, Dad. It means a lot."

He smiled back at me. "Good," he said. "I'll be back in a few minutes." He stood up and stalked off towards the bathroom.

"Honey?"

I jumped at the sound of my grandmother's voice, whipping my head around to see her standing before me. "Grandma?"

"What are you doing here, Charlotte? I thought you left hours ago!"

"We did," I explained, "but I'm back. My boyfriend got into a car accident."

"Oh, I'm so sorry, Dear," she said, taking my hand and sitting beside me in one of the uncomfortable hospital chairs. I couldn't help but wonder how much time she had spent there in the few days prior. "Why don't you explain everything to me?"

"Grandma, it's getting late," I told her, not really wanting to go through the whole story yet again. "Dad's here. You don't have to worry about me, and you should go get some sleep. I'll tell you everything sometime soon."

She nodded. "Okay, okay. You promise me you're alright here?"

"I promise." I paused. "How's Grandpa Henry?"

Her eyes lit up just at the mention of his name. "He's gonna be just fine," she said. "They're transferring him back to the nursing home on Tuesday."

"Oh, Grandma, that's wonderful!" I exclaimed, pulling her in for a hug. "I'm so glad he'll be okay. I was so worried!"

She smiled. "I was too," she said, rising to her feet. "But your grandpa, he's been through a lot, and he's always made it through. He'll make it through this, I know he will."

"Is he… Is he remembering any better?" I asked, playing with a loose floor tile with the tip of my black sneaker.

Her expression turned and I could feel a pit in my stomach. “They’re working on some things for him,” she said. “But nothing has changed there, not yet.”

“Oh,” I said. “Okay.”

“He’ll always be your grandpa, Charlie.”

“I know,” I muttered, returning my attention to the tile. “I know.”

She squeezed my hand. “It’s all gonna work out, Love. Don’t fret, okay?” I nodded and she blinked a few times, as if to clear her head. “Make sure you call me sometime and tell me all about this boyfriend of yours,” she said with a wink, her tone much lighter than before.

I smiled. “I will. His name is Jonah.”

“Jonah,” she repeated, as if analyzing his name. “I like that. Sounds strong.”

“He is, for sure,” I said. “And I’ll tell you everything soon. For now, though, you should go home and get some rest.”

She obliged, the bags under her eyes looking heavy. “I love you, Charlotte.”

“Love you too, Grandma. I’ll see you soon.”

A few moments later, my dad returned, shaking his hands dry. “Did I miss anything?”

“Grandma was just here, actually,” I said.

“You mean she still hasn’t gone home?” Concern lined his voice and he ran a nervous hand through his graying hair and toyed with his wire-rimmed glasses.

I never had the chance to answer him. A doctor appeared before us, wearing light blue scrubs under a white jacket with ‘Dr. Collins’ embroidered on the pocket. An extra pen was tucked behind her ear. “Are you Charlie Quinn?” she asked.

I nodded. “Is Jonah okay?”

“Why don’t you come with me?”

34

Lillian

Adagio, Maine, 1934

Ben and I were alone in the room. The rocking chair creaked gently as I shifted my weight front and back. My brother knelt at Mary's bedside, not daring to alter his focus for even a split second. Rain still drummed gently against the windows and no sunlight managed to peek through the curtains.

Mother, Father, and Dr. Flynn had stepped out of the room once Mary was stabilized. Ben and I exchanged occasional nervous glances, both of us wondering if our sister's life was still at stake. Before that day, I thought Ben knew everything. But even he didn't know the answer to this question.

"Ben?" I asked nervously.

He looked up at me, concern in his eyes.

"What if... What if..." my voice broke off as I held back tears.

"Don't," he said. "Don't think about that yet. We just have to wait and see what Dr. Flynn has to say."

I nodded and we both returned our focus to Mary, watching her intently, making certain she was still breathing. Within a few minutes, our parents re-entered the room, Dr. Flynn right behind. My mother's eyes were tearful, my father's usual stolid expression was laced with worry. Father hovered in the corner of the room by Mary's dresser as Mother tried to explain the situation to Ben and I. "Dr. Flynn thinks she'll be okay," she said, trying to dry her eyes. "He said it'll take time, but she's going to make it through."

"If all goes to plan, yes," he said. "She's stable for now, and I'll do everything I can to keep it that way." Dr. Flynn looked from my parents, to Ben, and then to me. "I believe the worst is over. Her pulse is returning to normal, but we must make sure to keep an eye on her and keep working on lowering her temperature."

My mother nodded. "Thank you," she said to him. "You saved my baby, my little girl."

"It's no problem at all," he replied, packing up his supplies and heading for the door. "Don't hesitate to send for me again if she worsens."

Dr. Flynn and my father left the room and headed down the hall. My own misty eyes met Mother's. "She'll be just fine," I said, beyond grateful that Mary had survived the ordeal.

She gave me a wistful look. "She'll be just fine," she repeated, and enveloped me in her warm arms.

"Lillian!" Charlotte's voice echoed from the doorway into Mary's room.

I jumped at the sound of her voice. "I'll be right back," I told Mother and Ben, rising from the rocking chair and leaving the room.

"Charlotte, what's wrong?" I asked, shutting the door behind me. "What are you doing here?"

"What am *I* doing here?" She asked me. "What were you thinking, running off on your own in the middle of the night?"

"Charlotte, I don't know what to say," I said, searching for the words. "I thought it would be best this way."

"In what way is *this* the best?" Her anger was escalating, and I began to worry she'd wake Mary. "You leave in the middle of the night, just after we made plans to go together? You abandon Henry and his little brother just because you couldn't wait a few more hours?"

"It's not about that, Charlotte! I wasn't trying to abandon you, I was trying to help!"

"Tell me how this, any of this, helped."

"You were so worried about coming home, I thought if I came alone you would be able to stay home, with Norman, safe," I said, gesturing towards the staircase, at the bottom of which I imagined Father would be skulking about.

A bewildered expression appeared on my sister's face. "You didn't think I'd come looking for you?"

"I left a note!"

"How was I supposed to know you even made it all the way home?" She asked, her soft-featured face growing redder by the second. "The storm last night was terrible, Lillian! Do you have any idea how dangerous lightning storms can be? You could've been swept out to sea and no one would ever know!"

"That's preposterous," I replied.

"What's preposterous is the fact that you spent so much time planning to run away for love, only to throw it all back in Henry's face when he tried to bring you home," Charlotte retorted, throwing her arms in the air.

"Charlotte, that's not fair. You know I love him."

"I do. But does he?"

"That's ridiculous, of course he does," I said. The longer I contemplated it, though, my confidence in the statement grew thinner.

Her voice became quieter, calmer. "Can you be sure? You left him, Lillian. Without a second thought."

"What did he tell you?" I asked, beginning to pace nervously through the hall.

"Nothing. But I overheard him telling Timothy they were leaving. I'm not sure where they planned on going." As I turned away, she took my hand and pulled me back to face her. "Lily, you…"

I interrupted her, suddenly overwhelmed. I thought I was going to suffocate as my breathing became labored and a harsh cry rose to the surface. "Oh, no. I've ruined everything, haven't I?" Tears stung my eyes.

Charlotte pulled me closer to her, muffling my cries. "Don't lose hope," she reminded me, her voice a calm whisper in my ear, "not yet." She gave a momentary pause. "But, Lillian?"

"Yes?"

"Never run away on me like that again. You had me worried beyond belief."

I nodded in agreement and rushed down the stairs, a waterfall of emotions cascading to the surface. I didn't know what to do, or say, or even think. Perhaps I had truly lost Henry forever. Perhaps I had thrown away the greatest part of my life. Perhaps I had made more than one grave mistake in just a single week.

I burst through the door, inhaling the fresh air, trying to catch my breath. I sat on the top stair, burying my head in my hands. The world was caving in around me. What had I done?

I don't know how long I sat there, on that porch, all alone. I do know that it was long enough for the rain to slow and the sun to poke through the clouds. I looked up to the sky, the sunshine leaking a drop of happiness, reminding me that it wasn't over. It couldn't be over.

My hair brushed against my neck, blown by a gentle autumn breeze that carried the beautiful chirp of a meadowlark along with it. I felt a surge of warmth inside, reminded of the song Henry and I had written. *Sing about the chirping of a songbird breaking through the silence of the morning,* he had told me. My glee quickly turned sour as I remembered what I had done, how I had shattered what we'd worked so hard to create between us.

Whistling.

Whistling? I looked up to find the source of the sound, knowing that it wasn't the song of any bird.

Standing under the tree just beyond the gate to my father's property was the very man I wished so desperately to see. My heart skipped a beat when I recognized him.

My eyes met his and he raised his eyebrows briefly, a gleeful smile spreading across his face. "You came back," I breathed, running down the stairs into his arms.

"I did," he said, then took a step away.

I stopped in my tracks. "Henry?"

"Lillian," he said, his bright smile disappearing, "why did you leave?"

"I-I thought I was doing what was best for my family," I replied in earnest. "Henry, I know I made a huge mistake-"

"I thought you trusted me." I could see the sense the betrayal in his eyes, and a pit formed in my stomach.

"I do!" I insisted.

"Then why did you leave?" he asked. "You didn't have to push me away," he said, taking my hands in his.

"I know, I just..."

"Lillian, I need to know that you trust me," Henry urged. "I can't go on thinking you might just leave again. I can't wake up to a cold, empty bed knowing that when I fell asleep I had you in my arms. I can't keep questioning whether you want to be with me, or if you'd rather run off and put yourself in danger."

"Henry, of course I want to be with you. I love you, more than anything!"

"I love you too, Lillian," he said. "But after everything I did to try to save you from... From *him*, and you just go running back into the thick of it all?"

"I wanted to care for my sister," I explained. "I thought the best way to do it would be to do it alone."

"But you don't *have* to do it alone, don't you see? You never have to do it alone, not anymore. You have me now," he said. He held up my chin and ran a hand through my hair. "I'll keep you safe."

"Henry, I'm so sorry. I never meant to hurt you." A tear ran down my cheek.

"You promise you'll never try to run off like that again?"

"Promise."

He pulled me in close and, suddenly, his lips met my own. In an instant, I knew I was back where I belonged, back with Henry. Back home.

35

Charlie

Adagio, Maine, 1990

"He's suffered a concussion, multiple contusions, and three broken ribs," the doctor explained. "We've already run multiple scans, and we're going to keep him overnight for observations. He's on plenty of pain medications right now, but he's conscious and wouldn't stop asking for you."

"He's going to be alright, though?" I asked, following her down a corridor lined with medical equipment, through a set of double doors and towards one of the rooms.

"With a little rest and TLC, he'll be good as new in a few weeks," she replied. She opened the door to Jonah's room and gestured for me to enter.

"Hey there," I said softly as I crossed the threshold. Yet again, I was greeted by those incessant beeps from all sorts of machines attached to Jonah in that uncomfortably sterile white room. I approached Jonah's bed, where he sat propped up against pillows, holding a tiny cup of water in his hand.

"I'll leave you two alone," said the doctor. "A nurse will be in to check with you shortly, Mr. Moore," she told Jonah.

I approached him slowly, each step heavy and burdened. "I'm sorry," I whispered as I reached him and our hands touched.

He furrowed his brow and tilted his head. "What? Why?"

"I shouldn't have left like that."

"Charlie, it's fine, you-"

"*I*," I said, shaking my guild-laden head.

"*You* what?"

"*I'm* the problem. It's my fault. I was being selfish, I didn't even think to leave you a note. I just ran off."

His expression grew serious. "You had good reason, you needed to come back here, your grandpa-"

"Not without talking to you first."

"What do you mean?"

"I *mean* that I can't keep putting myself first. I can't keep going like this. I can't keep forgetting that you're human, too, that you're also going through stuff, so much stuff…" I paused and wiped my tears with the sleeve of my sweatshirt. My lip trembled as I remembered all of the things I had learned about Jonah, all the trials of his life that seemed so big and terrifying compared to what I had been facing. His mother's alcoholism, her death, his life alone with his father…

"Charlie, look at me."

My attention snapped back to him, his familiar golden eyes drawing me back from those treacherous whirlpools of thought pulling me deeper, deeper, deeper.

"You aren't hurting *me* by feeling overwhelmed right now, you need to know that. You can't compare your own struggles with anyone else's. Not mine, not your friend's, not even your grandma's. You're allowed to hurt. None of this is your fault."

I nodded and gave a labored laugh, drying the last of my tears. "I love you," I said quietly. I leaned towards him and lifted one hand, my fingers brushing his face ever so slightly as I marveled at him, wondering how, even after a potentially fatal accident, he was still perfect.

"Then would you stop worrying and kiss me?" He whispered, leaning closer so his face was mere centimeters from mine. His breath, hot against my lips, sent a chill down my spine.

"Absolutely," I said, gently brushing my lips against his. He kissed me back, boldly, fiercely, relentlessly, as if there were no machines, injuries, or hospital beds in his way. I got closer to him, closer and closer, until there wasn't even room for air to fit between us.

The whole world was Jonah.

That is, until a knock came at the door and I had no choice but to scramble back to that little green chair by his bed. A nurse walked in, clipboard in hand. I smoothed my hair down and tried not to let her see how hot and bothered I had become in the few minutes prior.

"How are we feeling?" she asked, tying her shoulder-length red hair into a low ponytail. She looked at the rapidly beeping heart monitor, then back at Jonah, and finally to me, a slight smirk appearing on her face. She let out a small chuckle and pressed a few buttons. "Any more pain?" She put down her clipboard on a counter.

"Not that bad," Jonah said.

"He'll be okay, right?" I asked the nurse.

"His tests showed no signs of internal bleeding, and his concussion is minor," the nurse explained. "He should be just fine."

I let out a sigh of relief.

The nurse gave me a compassionate smile. "You seem like a great girlfriend," she said, and I blushed. "But, unfortunately, we don't allow visitors after ten."

I looked longingly at Jonah and a frown crept its way onto my face.

"She can't stay just a little longer?" he asked.

"I'm sorry, Mr. Moore," she said, taking some supplies from a shelf and moving about the room. She stopped when she reached the foot of his bed and looked at Jonah. "Rules are rules." She turned to me. "The painkillers are gonna kick in soon, and he needs to get some rest."

Jonah caught my eyes. "Goodbye." His voice was comically wistful.

I chuckled and stood up, taking his hand. "I'll see you tomorrow," I told him, giving him a kiss on the forehead. "I'll come and pick you up and we can go back to school together."

He smiled. “Okay,” he said softly. He leaned back against his pillows, clearly getting tired.

I headed out of the Jonah’s room and back towards the waiting room, where I saw my father approaching. “Hey, Dad. How’s Grandpa?” I asked, knowing he must have gone to visit his own father while he was here.

“Hi, Honey.” He yawned. “He’s stable. Doing a little better. Jonah?”

“He’s gonna be okay,” I said, relief in my voice. I took my jacket from my father’s arms and put it on. “I’ll pick him up tomorrow and we’ll go back to school together.”

“That’s great,” he said, standing. “Come on. Let’s get you home.” He wrapped an arm around me and we headed out to our cars.

I sat in the driver’s seat and leaned back, rolling my neck from side to side. Tomorrow we would go back to school. Jonah would call his dad about the car, and I would finally relax. We’d be back at school, back with our friends. My greatest worry would be the Music Theory final, not whether or not Jonah would survive the night. All would be well.

And it was.

The next day, I woke up at eight in the morning and said goodbye to my parents. I stepped outside and felt the bright, cold winter air chilling my cheeks and finally felt like everything would be okay again. I hopped into my Subaru and drove to the hospital, popping in Jonah's Bon Jovi tape and remembering how lucky I was to have my grandfather and boyfriend both alive.

36

Lillian

Adagio, Maine, 1934

I sat at my desk with a piece of paper and a pen, just as I had so many times before, ready to write a letter. Again.

This time, I had Henry by my side, helping me through every word.

Dear Father,

I know we have never gotten along. I know we have our differences, and I know our relationship is complicated. I shouldn't have run away. It was a trying time and I simply didn't know how to react. I hope you'll forgive me.

That said, I feel compelled to inform you that I've spoken with mother and we both think it best for me to move on. I will be living with Charlotte for a while. I believe it is time for me to learn to be independent and make my own choices. I know you find it best for me to simply stay with you and Mother until I find a husband, but I would rather be happy, and Mother agrees that this will be the best option for me right now.

I understand you do not approve of Henry. Maybe he doesn't have enough money, a high social standing, or a stable job. What he does have, though, is a strong heart, a will like no other, and a love for me. With time, I'm sure you'll come to understand why I've made the decision for us to live with Charlotte and Norman for a few months, until my twenty-first birthday.

I respect that you want to do what you think is best for me. And I hope that you will have the same respect for my decision.

Sincerely,

Lillian

"Sounds perfect," Henry said, kissing my forehead. "When do you plan on giving it to him?"

"Tonight," I told him. "After dinner."

"How do you think he'll take it?"

"I don't know," I said honestly. "He's been a bit unpredictable lately."

It had been a few days since Mary's seizure, and things were looking up for our family. Henry and Timothy had been coming by each day. Henry was able to spend time with me, and Timothy had become rather good friends with both Robert and Samuel. Father, who usually would've kicked out the Quinn brothers the second they breathed on our property, hadn't even threatened them in that time. I couldn't tell if he had somehow realized the fragility of life, or if he was simply too distracted by the situation, but he was growing less hostile with each passing day.

Still, I didn't want to take my chances. The possibility for him to lash out was too great, and I still felt a twang of fear in my chest whenever he would look into my eyes. Henry and I had spoken to Charlotte and Norman, and we had decided together that it would be best for us all to live together, at least until I was of age.

I stood up from my desk and looked at Henry. "Come on," I said. "I've got to help Mother finish preparing dinner."

We left my room and headed downstairs, past Mary's room, and into the kitchen. "Good evening, Mrs. Abbott," Henry said as we arrived.

"Hello, Henry dear," my mother responded, putting down her wooden spoon and hurrying over to him, hugging him tight and giving him a peck on the cheek. "How are you?"

"I'm doing well, thanks," he replied.

"And, Lily," my mother added in a hushed tone, "have you made a decision?"

"We spoke to Charlotte this morning," I explained. "She loves the idea."

"Splendid," said Mother. She turned to Henry. "Thank you for being so wonderful to my daughter." She picked up her spoon and resumed her mixing.

"Thank you," Henry replied, "for trusting and believing in me." He paused. "What of your husband? How do you think he'll take to this? He's not exactly fond of me."

"Lillian is nearly twenty-one," my mother explained. "We both knew she'd be leaving sooner or later…" She took a breath and placed a comforting hand on his shoulder. "I expect he'll be unhappy. But you two have my blessing, and you can be certain I'll be talking to him about the matter further."

"Thank you, Mother," I said. I opened the oven and pulled out a tray lined with seasoned chicken pieces, inhaling deeply. "These smell wonderful."

That night at dinner, Mary returned to her usual seat and Henry sat on my other side. Timothy joined Robert across from us. My muscles tensed when Father sat down at the head of the table, giving our guests a critical look. I took a deep breath, hoping he wouldn't change his mind about letting them share a meal with us after Mother and I fought so hard to convince him to allow it. Henry cleared his throat. "Thank you for letting me share dinner with your family, Mr. Abbott," he said, as if reading my mind.

Father pursed his lips and scratched his head of thinning hair. "Don't mention it," he replied coldly, refusing to make eye contact with Henry.

Henry and I exchanged nervous looks and didn't say much for the remainder of the meal. Occasionally, I noticed my father glaring in our direction, his eyes cold and sharp. "So, Father," I ventured, feeling forced to walk on eggshells in his disapproving presence, "how was work today?"

He took a bite of his chicken, his eyes still following Henry's every move. "It was a rather uneventful day," he replied.

"Well, Jacob," my mother said to him, "here at home we've been having a lovely time with Henry and Timothy." I was beyond grateful that she was on my side, but still I worried Father would lash out somehow.

He grunted softly. "So you have."

"Yes." I could tell she was trying to figure out the right thing to say as she continued. I played with the trim of the white tablecloth, doing everything in my power to avoid my father's gaze. "He's a delightful boy. Just took a job at the docks, from what I understand."

Henry nodded. "I love music," he said, "but I'd rather be able to provide for my future family." His hand slipped under the tablecloth and his fingers intertwined with my own. I tried not to let anyone see my blushing.

Father tilted his head to the side, his judging glare easing up ever so slightly. "I see."

"He's very caring, you see," my mother started up again. "And he's got lovely manners, he..."

Father cut her off. "I understand," he said, raising a hand.

"Um, I hear Ben is doing well in medical school," I said, trying to ease the tension.

Ben nodded, but no one said anything substantial for the remainder of the dinner. Henry and I exchanged the occasional nervous glance, but our lips were sealed. We didn't want to offend Father in any way before giving him the letter.

And then we gave it to him. After our meal was finished, and Mother began clearing plates from the table, I approached him, Henry standing beside me. "Father?"

He turned to me.

I handed it to him, my heart rapidly drumming inside my chest. “I’d like you to read this,” I told him. To my surprise, my voice didn’t waver. “I hope you understand.”

He gave me a quizzical look. “What is this?”

“Just read it.”

He unfolded the note and I watched his expression evolve from confused to downright enraged. “No,” he said, his voice unusually calm for the look on his face.

I was slightly taken aback. “Father, I-”

“I said, ‘no,’” he repeated, handing it back to me. He turned to Henry. “And you can leave my house,” he told him. “I won’t be asking again.”

He strutted off towards the kitchen.

“Father!” I called.

He stopped in his tracks.

“Father, I’m not asking for permission,” I said, trying to sound brave, despite my fear. Henry took my hand and looked at me, a comforting expression on his face. “I’m just letting you know,” I told my father.

My mother appeared in the archway between the kitchen and dining room. “Jacob?” she called out to him.

He whirled around to face her. “Have you given our daughter permission to move out of our home without so much as consulting me about it?”

My mother walked towards him slowly, speaking softly. “Yes, I did.” He opened his mouth to protest, but she continued. “I know you aren’t happy about it, but she deserves to have a chance at a happy ending.” She leaned in close to him and whispered something in his ear. Ever so slightly, his expression softened.

He took a deep breath and looked at me. “Fine,” he said. “But if you come back here all upset and heartbroken” – he shot a look at Henry – “you won’t be leaving again. Ever.”

I never thought I’d ever be compelled to hug my father, but in that moment, I did. I dropped Henry’s hand and rushed towards him, wrapping my arms around him as warm tears ran down my cheeks. “Thank you,” I breathed.

He took a step back, patted my back and didn’t say anything. I had never been more grateful; I had never been less terrified in his presence. I had never felt glad about anything he had ever said until that moment.

I pulled away and looked past him. My mother stood in the archway, drying a bowl with a light pink cotton towel. She smiled at me as I gave her a hug. "Mom, you-"

"Shh," she hushed. "I love you," she said.

"I love you too, Mom," I said, looking into her glistening eyes. "Thank you."

37

Charlie

Adagio, Maine, 1996

"Just like that?"

"Just like that," my grandmother replied. "To this day, I don't know what my mother told him, but something changed when she did."

I stood from the pink easy chair and stretched. I collected our teacups and walked them to the kitchen. "You and Grandpa ran away to Charlotte's then?"

"Well," she said, following me, "I had to collect my things and say goodbye to my brothers and Mary, but yes. Once we knew Mary would make a full recovery, we left for Charlotte's and lived there for the next couple of months.

Your grandfather got a job at the docks until we found the money to get married and find this place."

I smiled, feeling better and better about my engagement to Jonah. When he had proposed, I worried that we were too young, we weren't established enough, we'd barely be able to make ends meet. After talking to Grandma Lily, though, I remembered that none of that mattered. He was the only thing that mattered.

"That's amazing," I said. "You got your happy ending."

She chuckled. "My mother once told me, 'everyone should get a chance at a happy ending. If you get it, it's up to you to make it a dream come true.'"

I jumped when my Nokia phone started ringing in my purse. "Sorry. Let me go check that, Grandma," I said, heading back into the living room to the source of the sound. "Hello?"

"Charlie? It's Jonah."

"Hey, Jonah. What's up?"

"How's your grandmother? Did you guys get to talk?"

"Yes, yes," I told him. "She's doing just fine. What's wrong?" I asked, sensing a note of distress in his voice.

"Listen," he said, his voice hushed. "I just got to Adagio Nursing Home. I got a call a few hours ago that they're putting me on a new Alzheimer's case."

I said nothing.

"His name is Henry Quinn."

My muscles stiffened and a chill snuck down my spine. "You're sure?" I started walking laps around the sitting room.

"Yes."

"Okay," I said, trying to shake off the shock. "Okay. Um, you said you're there right now?"

"Yeah. I'm about to go see him."

"We're going right now," I said. I started gathering my things and waved to get Grandma's attention. She gave me a puzzled look.

"I'll be here," he said. "Love you,"

"Love you too." I hung up the phone and put it back in my purse, throwing on my jacket.

"What's going on?" Grandma asked as I helped her into her coat.

I shut off the lights and grabbed my keys. "Remember how I told you Jonah went into music therapy?"

She nodded.

"He just got a new patient," I explained. "It's Grandpa. Put your jacket on, we're going to go see him." I paused as a strange expression washed over her face, her eyes glistening with emotion. It was the same expression she wore when she told me about the first time she and Grandpa Henry met, their first kiss, the day they ran away. Her eyes grew wistful, the lines on her face softened, and a sad smile flashed across her face. "If you want to, I mean," I said, hoping I hadn't upset her.

"Okay," she said quietly.

"What's wrong? We don't have to go if you don't want to, I can call Jonah..."

"Nothing." She blinked away the tears forming in the corners of her eyes. "I remember some doctors mentioning that they were going to start music therapy with him, come to think of it."

We headed out the door, locking it behind us, and I unlocked my rickety little Volkswagen. "Hop in," I told her.

Grandma Lily's house was a thirty-minute drive from the nursing home. I always wondered why she hadn't chosen to move closer to Grandpa, but perhaps it was simply too hard for her, just as it was for us. Or, maybe, that little cottage by the sea that she had inherited from her older sister was just too dear to her to sell. I decided the latter was more likely.

"Do you want to listen to music?" I asked her, breaking the silent tension.

She shook her head. "If you want," she said.

I pulled out of the driveway without a word, wondering how I could make her feel better about seeing Grandpa. Maybe taking her to see him wasn't the right thing to do, after all. "You're sure you want to do this?"

She shifted in her seat. "Yes."

We drove past snow-coated trees, hills and valleys all covered in a fresh layer of wintry frost, jagged rocks lining the rough coast. I looked out to the sea for a moment, looking at the old dock, remembering Grandma's story. This was the very place she had first kissed my grandpa. She sat in the passenger's seat, looking out towards the dock's timeworn planks with clouded eyes.

I slowed down a bit, letting her watch the waves billow up and down, the edges of the surf lapping against the supports. "How did he propose?" I blurted out, immediately regretting my question.

She shook herself loose of the thousands of memories plaguing her mind and looked to me with her beautiful blue eyes, a tempest of icy blue flecked with gray, like the swell of the ocean beneath a stormy sky. "Oh, it was just lovely," she said.

"I'd expect nothing less," I replied, "from Grandpa."

My grandma gave a gentle, pensive smile. "Yes," she told me. "It was a few months after we had moved in with Charlotte, the morning of my twenty-first birthday. I had woken up early to sit on the porch and watch the sun rise over the ocean. It was the beginning of summertime, and I was listening to the cheerful bluebirds singing as I wrote poems in my little journal when your grandfather came outside."

38

Lillian

Adagio, Maine, 1935

"What are you doing up so early?" I asked, setting my journal down on the bench and giving Henry a gentle kiss on the cheek.

"Happy birthday," he said, ignoring my question.

"Thank you." I blushed, wondering how, after months of being with Henry, he still managed to give me butterflies with just the simplest smile.

He took my hands and helped me to my feet. "Of course." He paused for a moment, looking deeply into my eyes, his own filled with wonder.

"What?" I asked, suddenly conscious of his gaze.

He cleared his throat and collected himself, that giddy grin refusing to leave his face. "Nothing," he said. "You're just so beautiful."

I blushed again, but I was beginning to wonder if my life with Henry would lead me to have permanently rosy cheeks. I put an arm around his neck and rose to my tiptoes, brushing my lips against his as he pulled me into his familiar embrace.

"Come with me," he said, finally stepping away. He intertwined his strong fingers in my own and led me down the steps, off the porch and towards the dirt path leading away from the cottage.

"Where are we going?" I laughed.

"Why watch the sunrise from the porch when we can watch it on the dock?"

I smiled and followed him, the pair of us breaking into a swift jog, running along the familiar trail to the docks where we had spent so many perfect moments. My heart began to race. Something deep inside told me this would be another one of those moments.

The two of us finally arrived at the dock, the heels of our shoes clacking against the wooden planks. Laughing all the while, we kicked off our shoes and sat at the edge, letting the water lap at our bare feet. The sun moved slowly up into the sky, past the waves, casting a spectacular gradient of brilliant orange, pink, and yellow hues across the sky.

I looked at Henry as he stared off into the distance, his mind seemingly elsewhere. The streaks of yellow and pink reflected in his bright eyes. A warm feeling consumed me as I thought about the past few months that I had been so lucky to spend with him. I put my hand in his lap and he responded by putting an arm around my waist. "Isn't it beautiful?" He whispered into my ear, his warm breath against my neck reminding me of those butterflies that rested in my stomach, fluttering whenever he drew near.

I nodded in response. "This is already the best birthday I've ever had."

"I'm glad," he said, running his fingers through my hair and resting his forehead against my own. He kissed me gently and stood up, brushing himself off. He offered a hand and helped me to my feet. "I love you," he said.

"I love you, too," I replied.

"Really," he insisted, his tone steady and resolute. I smiled, reminded once more of his big heart, his great capacity for love. We were facing each other now, striking silhouettes against the backdrop of the radiant sky. The sun cast a gorgeous, bright glow on his face, and I couldn't help but be reminded of how I noticed the same thing on the night of our very first rendezvous, how the pale moonlight cast an iridescent reflection across his cheekbones. The thought of it made my heart flutter.

"Me too," I replied. "Really." *Doesn't he know how much I love him? Why does he sound so serious?* "Henry, what's wrong?"

He smiled at his feet, letting out a small chuckle. Henry reached out and took my hand in both of his. "When I met you, Lillian, I was struggling, with a lot of things."

I didn't realize I had been holding my breath, but I let it out just then, finally starting to realize just what Henry was about to do. I let him continue.

"I was trying to care for my brother, trying to make a living, somehow, alone."

I nodded, remembering our first encounter in the pub.

"And when I met you, all I wanted was you. I couldn't stop thinking about you, how kind you are, how beautiful you are…" He broke off.

I still couldn't think of what to say, so I remained silent as tears formed in my eyes.

"You're wonderful, Lily. I fell in love with you so quickly, it was terrifying. I didn't think it was a smart choice to keep chasing after you, because I was scared," he said. "I was scared of how deeply I cared for you, scared that I would never be able to show you…" He raised his free hand to my face, brushing his fingers against my cheek. "I know you were scared, too."

My lip trembled, and a stray tear slipped down my cheek, but he wiped it away with an adoring smile. "But in the end, none of it mattered," he continued. "All that mattered was you. Once I got to you, I knew everything else would fall into place… And it did."

He tucked a piece of my hair behind my ear and dropped his hand away, balancing himself as he descended to one knee. My heart soared beyond the clouds. "Let's keep it that way," he said, pulling a tiny box from his pocket. *The ring.* I was suddenly reminded of his status, thinking there was no way he could have afforded a real ring, but I didn't care. "Lillian Claire Abbott, will you marry me?" He opened the box to reveal the most beautiful piece of jewelry I had ever seen. A silver band wrapped around a clear and perfect diamond, the band weaving its way around the gem in a simple but elegant pattern.

I couldn't help but let out a gasp. "Henry, you…"

He smiled and explained. "Your mother gave it to me. It was your grandmother's."

"She gave… How did you… She…" I couldn't find the words to form a proper sentence, so I ignored my confusion with a shake of my head. "Yes," I told him, letting him slide the ring onto my finger. "Absolutely, yes!"

Before I had time to think, he whisked me into the air, and suddenly he was twirling me around just as he had on the night of our very first kiss, and my heart fluttered with joy all the same. I attacked him with a flurry of kisses, consumed by the utter euphoria cascading through my body.

He laughed and kissed me back, and when we finally pulled away from each other, he said, "I love you, Lily. I love you and I want to spend every minute of my life with you."

"Me too."

39

Charlie

Pine Ridge University, 1996

"First, I want to say congratulations to all of you for making it all the way through the fall semester!" Cedar's voice rang through the speakers, drowning out the rumble of the excited crowd of college students who had just finished the last day of classes before winter break.

"Give yourselves a hand!" They all screamed, almost simultaneously, clapping with gloved hands. I had only been out of college for two years, but somehow, being back on the lawn outside of Somerset Hall, I felt just as giddy as these eighteen-year-olds.

Cedar continued over their screaming. "Now," he said, "we are 'For Madeleine,' and for those of you wondering, my beautiful wife Maddy is right there, front row! Give her a round of applause, isn't she gorgeous?"

As the crowd cheered again, I looked at the beautiful blonde woman sitting in the red lawn chair beside me. We exchanged knowing smiles. "He flatters me," she said, adjusting her red scarf.

I smiled and nodded. Cedar and Madeleine had finally gotten back together during my sophomore year of college and married just a month after graduation. "I'm ever so grateful she came into my life, so I'd like to start off our show with a little number I wrote just for her. Take it away, Shane!"

The drummer, with his head full of ever-growing locks of blond hair, hit four starting beats on his cymbal before the band erupted into a melody that I remembered from one of the first times I had ever heard them perform. Cedar had changed the lyrics to honor his wife, rather than beg for her forgiveness, but the tune remained the same. A huge smile found its way to my face as my eyes wandered to the bass player, watching my boyfriend of six years back up on the stage, doing what he loved.

We had moved in together after college in a town not too far from where I grew up. He started working for his father's music therapy business, and I had just gotten my first teaching job. Things were going well.

All he needs to do now is put a ring on that finger, my mother's voice echoed in my head. I shook my head, trying not to think about how all she wanted was for me to get married. A few years ago, she fought the idea of me even dating anyone, but Jonah had stolen her heart just as he did my own. Now, she just couldn't wait for him to be a part of the family.

I knew, deep down, that she was right. We had been together for six years. I only hoped that he was waiting so long to ask me because he wanted it to be incredibly romantic, as he knew I'd been dreaming of our engagement for years. However, when my mother pushed, something ached inside of me, and I prayed that I was right, that he really was just planning something epic, something beautiful.

I had no idea what was about to hit me.

Maddy and I rose to our feet when they finished their first number, clapping and shouting all the while. Jonah waved to me from the back corner of the stage and winked. He tightened his bandana, which he pulled from the back of our closet just for this reunion show.

"Thank you, thank you!" Cedar shouted into the microphone. "And now, I have to recognize that, while I do have the most beautiful wife in the world, I'm not the only guy on this stage who loves his lady."

I half-expected Declan, one of the guitarists, to step forward and confess his love for Cedar's younger sister, Natalie. I chuckled at the thought of the two of them tussling onstage, while Shane laughed in the background and Jonah tried to pull them apart.

Instead, though, Jonah stepped forward and handed his bass to Otto, who replaced his guitar with the new instrument. Cedar handed him the mic and he cleared his throat. "Charlie," he said.

I was frozen in place. Was he actually calling me up on the stage? What was he going to make me do? He knew I loved to perform, but rock shows were his area of expertise. I was jolted back to reality when Maddy pushed me forward, and I stepped up onto the rickety wooden stage, the same one the band had played on the first time I had ever seen them.

A familiar melody started playing in quietly in the background, and I recognized it immediately. A tiny, vocalized laugh escaped my lips when I realized it was our favorite Bon Jovi song.

Jonah looked at me and gave a warm, sentimental smile. "I love you so much," he said.

The crowd let out a communal chorus of "aww."

I nodded and heat rushed to my cheeks.

"I've loved you since the day we met, when you were all timid and covered in coffee, and I've loved you every day since," he said, beaming. "I should have proposed two years ago, when we spent that weekend at the beach, but I just couldn't let your mother get what she wanted so easily."

I laughed through the tears that had started to burn my eyes. I tried to look him in the eyes without erupting into a crazed flurry of a thousand different emotions as he rested one knee on the stage.

"Instead, I thought I'd do it on our terms. We're done with college now. We have an apartment. We have jobs. We're regular adults, unlike some people I know," he said, giving a comedic gesture to Cedar, to which the crowd chuckled. "We're ready now… And I want to marry you, Charlotte Quinn. Would you do me the honor?"

"Of course, yes, absolutely!" I cried, not even giving him the chance to show me the ring before throwing my arms around him and pulling him in for a kiss.

He laughed. "Don't you want to see it?"

I nodded silently, and he opened the tiny velvet box. "My great-aunt's ring," I breathed, examining the gold ring. It was just as I remembered – just after my great-aunt's passing, the ring had been handed down to my grandmother. In my youth, I would sit at the edge of her bed and marvel at the object, the brilliant diamond reflecting the light spilling from the open window.

Jonah gave a proud nod.

"Wait, I don't understand, how..."

"Your father gave it to me. Said your grandma gave it to him a few years ago, before you guys moved away and lost touch. She wanted you to have it. Something about keeping family bonds alive. Here," he said, slipping it onto my finger, calloused from years of violin-playing. "From what I understand," he continued, "it was your great-aunt's ring, and her mother's before that, and before that it belonged to *her* mother... Or maybe it was her aunt's, I'm not sure. You're much better at this stuff-"

I couldn't take it anymore, and I interrupted his babbling with a huge kiss. "It's perfect," I told him. "You're perfect."

He lifted me into the air as the band reached the chorus of our song. The crowd erupted into applause. I was sure they were all very happy for us, but it couldn't compare to how I felt in that instant. No one was happier. Not a soul.

40

Lillian

Adagio Nursing Home, 1996

"That's a beautiful story," I said to my granddaughter as she pulled into a parking space at the nursing home. Anticipation flooded my veins as I thought about seeing Henry yet again. Every day, I made the same trip. Every day, I saw him. Every day, a tiny piece of me was crushed.

"Thanks," she replied, gathering her auburn hair into a little bun atop her head. I watched the gold band of her ring glint in the sunlight as she did so, and I felt warm inside. My older sister's diamond ring suited my granddaughter perfectly. I smiled in admiration, thinking of how alike she was to her namesake. She pulled her keys out of the ignition and her eyes met mine. "Ready?"

I nodded, taking a deep breath and stepping out of the vehicle. *You can do this*, I told myself. *You've done it a hundred times before*. I tried not to think about how each time was harder than the last as Charlotte and I walked slowly up the ramp, hand in hand, and in through the sliding glass doors of the nursing home. "Hi, there, Lillian," a woman at reception said to me.

"Hi, Lucy," I responded. Charlotte gave my hand a gentle squeeze as I headed up to sign in at the reception desk.

"He's actually in a session right now," explained Lucy.

Charlotte interjected. "He's with Jonah Moore, from Moore Music Therapy, right?"

Lucy nodded.

"He's my fiancé," Charlotte continued. "Could we go in?"

"I'm sorry, Miss," she said, "but you're going to have to wait until the session is over. I'll have someone come get you right away." She spun around in her swivel chair and picked up a phone.

I put my arm around my granddaughter's waist and led her to a waiting area. "We'll just wait here," I told her.

Charlotte complied. We only waited for a few minutes before I noticed her head perk up from behind the magazine she had been mindlessly flicking through. "Jonah!" she said.

I looked up to see a man approach and kiss her. He wore a pair of black slacks and a big smile on his face. His wavy brown hair was neatly combed. I sized him up and down, trying to figure out if I liked him. From what I heard from Charlotte's stories, he was a perfect gentleman, and he clearly made her very happy; that was enough for me to approve.

"You must be Mrs. Quinn." My granddaughter's fiancé nodded in my direction and offered his hand. "I'm Jonah."

"Oh, I've heard all about you," I said, taking it.

"Good things, I hope," he replied. After a pause, he continued. "Come with me."

Charlotte and I followed him down a narrow hallway, a hallway I knew all too well. My breath hitched as we approached the doorway to his room, and I readied myself to see him through the window, sitting alone in the room as he always was when I would come by. Instead, Jonah continued down to the end of the hallway, where he gently pushed open a door. He grabbed Charlotte's wrist.

"Stay out here with me for a minute," he whispered to her. "Mrs. Quinn, go ahead in," he told me.

I took a tentative step into the room, lined with thin blue carpet and beige-colored walls. "Henry?" my voice echoed in the near-empty room.

He didn't pay attention to me. He was facing towards the wall, sitting at a piano in the back of the room, inspecting the keys intently, all of his attention focused on the instrument.

"Henry." I said it louder this time, more deliberately.

His attention snapped away from the piano, and he looked at me, his green eyes empty.

"Henry, it's me."

"Who are you?" he grumbled. "Do I know you?"

"It's Lillian," I said, swallowing hard. I willed myself not to cry as my stomach tied itself in knots. *You do this every day. Stay strong.*

He grunted and turned back to the piano. "Can you play something for me?" I asked.

"Play what?"

I walked over to the piano and sat beside him on the bench. I took in a sharp, labored breath, remembering how many hours we had spent together on piano benches in the past. I rested my fingers over the keys and exhaled slowly. "Do you know this song?"

I pressed down on the keys, letting the familiar chords resonate in my body. My heart sped up. I would always remember our song. I prayed the same went for Henry.

He tugged at his hair with his hands. I looked away from the piano keys, trusting my fingers to play the old melody properly, and gazed at Henry. His eyes had filled with tears. "What is this?" He asked, his voice cracking.

"It's our song, Henry," I said, trying to hide how my heart had begun to shatter.

He settled down and watched my hands intently. He rested his fingers over the keys above my own and began to play it himself. A hot tear ran down my cheek and I began to hum the melody that we had composed together one night in my father's parlor, years and years ago. It rang true; the achingly beautiful melody echoing in my heart the same way it had on that fateful night.

His fingers glided naturally across the keys, as if he had never stopped playing even after so many years. I kept humming, watching his expression change as he realized he knew how to play the song. He looked back and forth from the piano to me, and, suddenly, he stopped playing altogether.

"What is it?"

"Lillian," he whispered. He looked at me and tucked his hand in my hair, behind my ear, just like he used to when we were young. "Lillian, Lillian," he repeated, again and again, his voice breaking as his eyes searched mine for some nostalgic sense of familiarity that he knew was hidden within the depths of his distorted memory.

I nodded, my mind in a frenzy. "Yes, Henry," I said, glee in my voice and tears in my eyes. *He remembers. He doesn't know he remembers, but he does.* "It's me. It's Lillian."

I leaned towards him and kissed him softly. When I pulled away, I looked at him intently. His face hadn't changed. He still had the same sharp jawline, the same high cheekbones, those same green eyes that I had fallen in love with over and over again, every morning when I woke up beside them, every morning for nearly fifty years.

They hadn't changed. They were duller, sure. He didn't have the same fire, the same drive, the same energy he once had.

But he was still Henry.

I could see it in his eyes. I could see him in there. That man I devoted my life to, he was trapped inside an empty shell, but I knew, deep down, he was there. He always would be. And I would always be beside him, no matter how much it hurt.

"I love you," I reminded him. "I'll always love you, Henry."

Something flickered across his eyes just then. Maybe it was a trick of the light. Maybe I was wrong.

Maybe he remembered.

I couldn't help but think that he was coming back to me, little by little. Those broken pieces of my heart began to merge together again. His mind may not have remembered me, not yet. But I knew his heart always would.

Acknowledgements

Thank-you first to my incredible family for being my biggest supporters throughout the journey of *Our Song*. Thanks to my amazing readers, to those who weren't afraid to tell me when something didn't sound quite right, and to those who were. You all know who you are, and I'm forever grateful for your patience, perseverance, and loyalty. Without you, this dream would not have become reality. I would never have been able to do this without the help and support of my high school English teachers; they've been with me through the best and worst of my writing, whether they realize it or not. Thank-you to Lukáš Dlutko and Pexels for the incredible photograph used on the cover. And, finally, thank *you,* reader, for taking the time to purchase and read my first novel.

About the Author

KATE ROWAN is the pseudonym of Katelyn Rehatchek, author of *Our Song* and college student from Northeastern Pennsylvania, where she is about to begin her sophomore year as an English Education major. When she isn't reading or writing, Kate enjoys participating in theatrical productions and playing the saxophone. She lives with her adoring parents, Don and Chrissy, younger brother, Josh, and cat, Rascal. It is her biggest dream to inspire her future students to find and explore their artistic passions.